One Little Chance

REBECCA JO
JACKSON

One Little Chance

A CHRISTMAS NOVELLA

SWEET RIVER SERIES
BOOK THREE

REBECCA JO JACKSON

Playlist

I always make a playlist for each book I write. Below is what I listened to while writing One Little Chance— to me this is the soundtrack of the story, what played in the background while Sophia and Jordan fell back in love. Listen along if you'd like.

1. Christmas Makes Me Cry by Kacey Musgraves
2. Same Boat by Lizzy McAlpine
3. What a Time by Julia Michaels
4. Winter Song by Sara Bareillies & Ingrid Michaelson
5. the way i used to by Kelsea Ballerini
6. Chasing Shadows by Alex Warren
7. I miss you, I'm sorry by Gracie Abrams
8. Maroon by Taylor Swift
9. if we never met by John K (feat. Kelsea Ballerini)
10. There's a Reason by Wet
11. Taxi by EXES
12. get over you by Dylan Conrique
13. What if I Love You? by Gatlin
14. Still by Niall Horan
15. It's Nice to Have a Friend by Taylor Swift
16. Francesca by Hozier
17. Falling Like the Stars by James Arthur

18. Your Bones by Chelsea Cutler
19. I Want to Live With You by Alex Lahey
20. Home by Good Neighbours
21. All This Time by Norah Jones
22. Always Been You by Shawn Mendes
23. This Christmas by Ingrid Michaelson
24. This Love (Taylor's Version) by Taylor Swift
25. What Are You Doing New Year's Eve? By Norah Jones

You can also find this playlist on Spotify.

For the recklessly hopeful.

And for Jenna.

Prologue

DECEMBER 23RD, 2023

I could still remember when I first fell in love. How I fell in love slowly, like growing up, over years and years. Snow was falling outside this December morning as I peeked out my living room window, little kisses blown by Jack Frost. Fire crackles in the fireplace warming my little house.

I had waited for this day since I was a little girl. It had me reflecting on *love*.

When I first fell in love, it sounded like my childhood best friend, Jordan, laughing my name, "Sophie," as my chestnut hair fell across my eyes. It felt like him brushing it behind my ear.

I watched the snow pile up in the park across the street, thinking about how heartbreak also sounded like Jordan's voice, holding back tears as he pleaded, "Sophie," his hazel eyes on me as I walked away at eighteen.

I let the thick white curtain fall back over the window, rubbing my arms for warmth. I moved into this house only a year ago. Last December, back when I broke the promise I'd made to myself to never return to Sweet River.

Chapter 1

DECEMBER 24TH, 2022

It was icy the day before Christmas. My breath came out in little puffs as I yanked my suitcase from the back of the silvery blue Corolla I parked outside my mom's house. Since my parents' divorce, she'd changed her last name back to her maiden name, Viletti, and moved into this little house my brother and I lovingly called the Viletti Villa.

She had apologetically admitted over the phone a couple of years ago that she was renting a place a few houses down the street from Jordan—*my ex.*

Though *ex* didn't quite communicate everything Jordan Silk was to me.

He was my childhood crush, my high school sweetheart, my best friend. Like a favorite jacket that fit just right no matter how I grew over the years. The voice I would fall asleep to on the phone when we were apart on family vacations. A face I searched for in the stands during track meets, to remind me that I was a winner no matter the score.

Growing up down the street from him in my family's old house had been a gift I used to use to my advantage, walking over on the weekends and pushing the boundaries on my curfew until the very last possible second. *Now, eight years since our breakup, in*

Mom's new house, the proximity to his family's place made staying at Mom's house stressful, I bitterly thought as I slammed my car door. I froze at a familiar sound.

Oh no. Christmas carolers. *It was December 24*. I knew, Jordan's family, the Silk's traditions.

Christmas lights blinked to life across this street. I tried to hurry, throwing a couple of bags over my shoulder and grabbing my rolling suitcase to scurry up the driveway. The achingly familiar voices grew closer.

When the heel of my boot hit a patch of ice, my legs slid under me. *Ouch*. I landed on my behind. Chilly water soaked into my jeans as my face blazed red.

The carolers were far enough away not to witness the fall but close enough that as I hobbled back up, they arrived in front of the driveway just in time to see me awkwardly trying to pull my coat over my soaked bottom.

I doubted Jordan realized this was my mother's house. Or, in this small town...he totally knew. But *she* hadn't dumped him their freshman year of college, cut off all communication, and married someone else. Caroling in front of her was an entirely different situation than caroling in front of *me*.

As Jordan and his family sang, "We Wish You a Merry Christmas," I froze in place. Would it be rude to turn and bolt? Should I sing along? Who would I look at? *Do not look at Jordan's face. Do not look at Jordan's face*. Though staring at his beefy, quarterback shoulders wasn't exactly a comfort either.

My mom's hunter-green front door creaked open before they sang the last few lines. She rushed out across the front porch, clapping for the end of the performance. I gave her something between a smile and a pained wince.

Everyone merrily wished us a Merry Christmas, and Jordan's eyes latched onto mine. Two puzzle pieces connected. Like our connection was unavoidable. He stepped back in surprise at my presence.

His hazel eyes were puffy, rimmed in red. His shoulders

hunched. His sandy hair was a mess. He was hurting. Something had happened.

After all this time, my entire body was reflexively drawn to wrap hurting Jordan in my arms, to soak up his sorrow like a sponge. I bit back the urge to reach out to him because I'd erased those rights out of my life.

He pulled his gaze away quickly, shaking his head as if standing there with tear-stained eyes singing Christmas songs in front of his ex-girlfriend was just too much.

I watched his family walk away, his grandmother rubbing his back as they strolled back home. Noting, with a glimmer of something recklessly close to hope, that his girlfriend of the past couple of years, Emma Brown, was *not* with him.

The Silks started singing "Oh Holy Night" as they walked further down the street. It used to be me all huddled in my fluffy coat singing along with them, giggling through the cold.

My mom swung her arm around my shoulder clutching my puffy white coat. "Oh, babe, welcome home."

I cuddled underneath a chunky knit blanket on my mom's living room couch as she shuffled around the kitchen only separated from the living space by a half kitchen bar. The whole house smelled of Mom's spaghetti Bolognese.

It had been eight years since I was the one bundled up with Jordan's family. His mom wrapped her red scarf around my neck to keep me warm as we sang Christmas songs under the glow of the neighborhood's twinkle lights. I'd been singing along with them from the time I was a little girl in pigtails until I was a senior in high school. It was *my* Christmas tradition, too. Hearing it outside my mom's windows as she brewed me a cup of tea felt like turning the pages of a scrapbook I'd kept locked away for years.

Jordan was as vital a piece of my childhood as the streets of my neighborhood. His dining room table showed up as often as my own in memories. His dad beamed with pride at my track meets and softball games as often as my own father.

It was difficult when my world—my family—broke apart to understand which pieces were painful memories that cut, and which were safe to hold in my hands. *Better to toss them all away,* eighteen-year-old me had thought. A bright-eyed freshman in college. *I can throw myself into a new life.*

Mom laughed at the Silks encore performance booming across the street waking from my thoughts. Her gaze focused on me.

"What're you thinking about?" she asked me, an eyebrow raised at my quietness.

"Oh...thinking about Christmas Eves from forever ago." I attempted a small smile.

Ex *was* such an inadequate way to describe him. Jordan was the boy who had shown up outside my house when I was fourteen years old on Christmas Eve night, knocking on my door urgently like there was some kind of Christmas emergency.

I ran fuzzy socked to the door, sliding on the hardwood floors. "Jordan." I giggled as the front door swung open.

He stood tall in the doorway with bright eyes, eagerly holding mistletoe over his head. "I found some mistletoe," he whispered shakily.

My cheeks flushed. "Mistletoe?"

"I thought...for Christmas..." My always confident Jordan was now nervous at the closeness of my awkward teenage self. Limbs too long, hair too frizzy, but still he looked at me like I was perfect. His eyes were on my lips.

"We should kiss, huh?" I grinned, mustering confidence for the two of us. "Traditions and all?" We'd been circling around a kiss all year. Waiting, nervous, hopeful.

The sky was such a deep blue it was almost black overhead. Frosty air blew in around him.

He nodded, his eyes wide in surprise as if he hadn't really believed his plan would work. He swallowed, placing his free hand against my lower back. I raised onto the tips of my toes in my fuzzy red socks, and he bent down, his tall athletic self leaning down to meet me.

Two lips met for the first time on a Christmas Eve night. His mouth was cold and tentative, tasting like hot chocolate.

It was perfect.

I touched my lips years later. That kiss was still a mark on me like a tattoo no amount of heartbreak could ever wash away. *So much more than just an ex.*

I watched the sky go dark out the window blinds, the Christmas lights hanging on the houses growing more prominent in the night. I couldn't stop thinking about Jordan's red-rimmed eyes. I had no right to know what happened. It had been eight years since we'd last spoken. But, even after all this time, I hadn't figured out how to stop caring about him.

I'd thought of him countless times—we'd spent far more years together than we'd ever spent apart. I'd wonder how his dream of building homes with his father was going. If he still ran in the mornings like we used to do. If he'd fallen in love with Emma. If he ever missed me.

Now, after seeing him face to face tonight, my mind was spinning. The last time I'd been in the same city, let alone on the same street as Jordan, my life was completely different.

My younger brother, Orlando, and I grew up in a tight-knit family of four: framed photos on the wall, homemade peppermint candy in the kitchen, and picking up relatives at the airport. Mom and Dad had been high school sweethearts, getting married fresh out of college and having me in their early twenties.

I grew up to the sound of them giggling together in the kitchen while my mom made Nonna's handed-down pasta recipes. My dad asked me, "Doesn't Mama look beautiful today?" as the scent of garlic and tomato filled the house. A soft, sweet equilibrium to my world.

But then, like a favorite song coming to an end, a hot July night before I left for college, my mom and dad sat Orlando and me down in the living room around our old wooden coffee table.

"We're getting a divorce," my dad announced as if proposing a new plan at a business meeting instead of telling his kids that their two parents, the four of us, were now broken into separate pieces. Our little world fractured, cracked, broken for good.

My voice was wobbly as I said, "I can't believe this."

My parents were at a loss for how to comfort me when they couldn't even comfort themselves. It was so quiet, so tense, I could still hear the fan overhead and feel the sweat on the back of my neck.

"I can't believe this," I repeated to Orlando later that night. My voice was just as broken, the hurt still raw. Neither of us could sleep that night, so we sat together in the hallway between our rooms until the early hours of the morning.

"Really, Sophie?" Orlando whispered gently. His hair was a chestnut color that matched mine with the same freckles across his nose.

"Really." I tugged at the gray carpet under my legs.

I was shocked. Until I wasn't. Packing my bags for college suddenly felt like stumbling upon clues in a case—everything was proof of my parent's marriage coming undone.

Cardboard boxes Mom got me and helped pop open while Dad was away on yet another work trip.

Packing clothes I opened on a quiet Christmas morning that my Dad hadn't even realized Mom bought. He was distracted and moody that whole day.

I tiptoed through the kitchen to steal a few bowls and spoons for my new dorm room, wondering when Mom and Dad stopped giggling in there.

The house was quiet as I packed, I felt myself noticing it for the first time. Quiet was our normal for the past several years, wasn't it? Mom and Dad's old jokes were buried under years of distance.

"When did you realize?" Mom asked me over the phone weeks

later, when I collapsed into tears demanding to know if Dad had left her for someone else.

How could I miss it? Turned into a frantic, how much could I miss?

Now, I was back in Sweet River, my hometown, in Mom's Viletti Villa, sitting on a plush green couch instead of the worn-in red sectional I grew up with. So many things were different, but not everything.

Time taught me that some things don't change. Visiting home still smelled like Mom simmering something tomato-based on the stove. Tonight was one of those nights as garlic and fresh tomatoes filled the house. And she still hung big wreaths on the windows and red bows on the kitchen cabinets. And it was still my family's voices that filled my ears on nights like these.

I wished I could go back and whisper in my eighteen-year-old self's ear, *things might've shattered, but some pieces would always be yours.* But she'd figure it out all in good time.

Mom was humming in the kitchen when Orlando burst through the door Christmas Eve night with a big, lush tree. Mom and I ushered him in, guiding him to a spot to place it. It put the artificial two-footer to shame.

Orlando was a junior in college and home for Christmas break.

"I saw Mom's tiny one was still around and thought it was time she upgraded!" Orlando said, eyeing the new real eight-foot tree proudly. It made the living room smell like pine.

I'd spent the first few Christmases after my parents split with my ex, Tyler's family. Each of us in our family tentatively tried something different like walking on unsteady ground. Mom went on a cruise that first year. Orlando went to the snowy mountains with some family friends. Until we finally started spending Christmas with the three of us again—Mom, Orlando, and me. We haven't looked back since. Repairing our pieces like a fallen ornament, not quite the same as before, but still beautiful and in some ways, even better.

Mom bought the two-foot Christmas tree that first year the three of us celebrated together again. It became our family tree for years. It made us giggle, and we loved how the big ornaments looked on it. Mom was happier, lighter, even better now after the break.

"Tiny Tree still needs a place," I said as Mom and Orlando fluffed the new tree. I glanced around the room, searching for a spot.

Mom offered, "How about in your room, by the window?"

I smiled at Mom referring to the guest room as *my room*. In her mind, no matter what happened, Orlando and I were her two kids and wherever she lived was our home. I carried Tiny Tree into the guest room, setting it on the table by the window. I opened the curtains, so it shared its twinkle lights with the neighborhood. I peeked out to see kids running around the neighborhood pink-cheeked, giggling, and high on Christmas.

I was home. I felt like someone had wrapped a blanket around my shoulders after a long time in the cold.

Chapter 2

DECEMBER 25TH, 2022

Christmas morning tasted like hot coffee with cinnamon sprinkled atop and sounded like Mom and Orlando giggling over silly holiday memories while bacon sizzled in the frying pan. The new Christmas tree was aglow in the corner of the living room.

I sat at the round oak kitchen table with fuzzy red and green socks on while Orlando grinned at me through sleepy eyes.

"Little us would judge older us for eating breakfast before presents," Orlando said as he poured himself more coffee.

"I miss little you trying to sneak into the living room at all hours of the night to catch Santa in the act." Mom sighed wistfully at the memory.

"Look where we are now," I said, before taking a hot sip. "I'm back in Sweet River getting my own place. You're in college."

"I wonder where we'll be even a year from now." Orlando came and sat beside me at the table. That question gave my heart little anticipatory flutters, like turning the first pages of a new story.

"Oh, oh, speaking of little you. Did we tell you who we ran into yesterday?" Mom asked Orlando while pointing toward me with the spatula.

"Who?" he asked. The smell of bacon made my stomach growl.

I hid my face in my hands. "Jordan. And his family. They came caroling."

Orlando busted out a laugh, leaning back in his chair. "Of course, the Silks came a caroling."

"*Jordan.*" My eyes went wide as I said his name. "Who I haven't seen in forever, shows up in our driveway right after I've slipped on ice getting out of the car—"

"Orlando, I walk out there and the first thing I see is Sophia's wet bum like she dipped her tush in a bucket of water," Mom said as she moved the cooked bacon onto a plate with a fork.

"Why would she ever dip her tush in a bucket of water?" Orlando squinted at Mom.

"I hid it with my jacket!" I dropped my hands to the table. "I don't know how you saw a thing, Mom."

"The jacket was drenched, too. It was your entire backside," Mom said softly as if trying to gently tell me the truth.

I sighed, standing up and walking over toward the stove. "It was awkward. I'm soaked. He's caroling. He was avoiding looking straight at me."

"Imagine how he feels—he hasn't seen his elementary, junior high, high school sweetheart in years. Then there he is wearing his fluffy coat and singing Christmas songs in front of her."

"How'd you know he was in a fluffy coat?" I snatched a piece of bacon and popped it into my mouth.

"I grew up with Jordan, too. I was there for all of it. Of course, he was in that old giant coat of his that used to be his dad's." He crossed his arms. "Yeah, you might've been soaked. But you also don't want to run into the girl that got away in your old fluffy coat."

"I've always loved that coat," I admitted. I used to wear it more than he did.

After we opened presents, Nonna and Nonno came over so Nonna and Mom cooked up their classic Christmas manicotti. Later, while the rest of the family watched Christmas movies, I was going through old cardboard boxes and plastic tubs with Mom in her cramped garage, trying to collect anything I might want to take with me to my new house.

It was like going through a scrapbook of our childhood in objects. Old school projects, favorite stuffed animals, and outgrown shiny yellow rollerblades. Mom and I both got misty-eyed and refused to ever part with it. Did I need a box of old stuffed animals? No. Was I absolutely bringing along my old Lamby and Hop Hop? Yes.

When I found an old, yellowed plane ticket at the bottom of a box. I pulled it out and read the note scrawled over it.

Merry Christmas, Sophie. Come play in the snow with me? Love, Jordan.

Suddenly, I wasn't standing amongst old boxes anymore. Instead, I was back in my memories, seventeen again and giddy over Christmas break.

We were running late. Jordan, his parents, sisters, brother, and me the bonus tagalong, all crammed into their shiny red suburban speeding along to the airport.

"Check-in is in..." His mom, Pat, rubbed her forehead defeatedly, not finishing her sentence.

"I can get us there." His dad, Carson's, voice was as tight as a bottlecap. Jordan and I exchanged a glance, the two of us happily squeezed in together in the backseat, fingers laced. We ignored his sister, Jenna, shaking her head at us.

"These two." She nudged Sarah on the shoulder and nodded toward us.

"The lovebirds couldn't care less that we're going to miss our flight." Jordan's brother, Cody, patted him on the shoulder from the backseat.

He was right.

Checking our bags and fumbling through the security line was chaotic and noisy, but it was as if the stress around us couldn't reach Jordan and me in our little fortress of happiness. Together we could make anything a joke, always taking turns being each other's sunshine.

We jogged after his dad through the airport, Jordan's hand never dropping mine with "All I Want for Christmas," vibrating through the airport speakers.

We arrived at the gate right on time to hear an announcement through the speakers, "Flight 2829 to Ruidoso has been delayed by two hours. Please speak to the gate assistant if this interferes..."

Carson turned to our motley crew squeaking to a stop on the glossy airport tile. He broke into a laugh. It rippled through all of us. After working so hard to barely make it on time...we were now stuck in the airport for the next two hours. Everyone moaned and slapped their hands across their heads, but I liked being stuck with Jordan and his family. They could extend my time with Jordan all they wanted.

"Now we have time to stock up on snacks, I guess." Pat shrugged, gesturing toward the tiny airport market behind us.

Under the fluorescent lights, the airport shops still hung twinkle lights and positioned Christmas trees with shiny red and green bulbs. I meandered through the glossy racks of magazines with

Jenna and Sarah when Jordan snuck his around my waist holding a cup of coffee out before me.

"One cinnamon coffee," he said. I never did have to ask.

"Just what the doctor ordered." I gratefully wrapped my hands around the cup, taking a whiff of the nutty, sweet scent.

"I feel like at this time of year you're basically eighty percent cinnamon coffee. It worries me," Jordan said playfully furrowing his brows. His jawline now more chiseled than when we grew up.

"Yet you're buying them for me unprompted?" I shrugged and took a warm sip.

"You know this boy can't resist giving you whatever you want." Jenna grinned, holding up a pinky. "You have him wrapped."

"It's bad. He's been obsessed with trying to find you the perfect Christmas gift," Sarah said as she flipped through a baking magazine. "It has to be perfect."

"Is that true?" I cocked a head toward Jordan, my cup still warm in my hands.

His cheeks went pink. "Well, yeah, I've been stumped. I want it to be just right."

"I relate." I stepped closer to him. "I've had trouble finding the right gift for you too."

I'd almost bought several things, but it seemed I'd do what I'd done the past several years which was wait until the very last minute to finally settle on something that was only good enough. When we were fourteen, I'd given him Cowboys stadium tour tickets that I'd won on a radio contest I'd followed along religiously to win. That was the only gift I'd ever felt was sufficient. Every other one had lived in its shadows since.

"You two crack me up. I'm sure you could buy each other some random junk from one of these airport gift shops and be over the moon because it was coming from each other," Jenna mused as she tucked a magazine back on the rack.

Jordan's eyes sparkled with an idea. "What would you get me from here?"

I glanced around the cramped shop. "I have no idea. What would you get me?"

His smile spread. "I don't know, but I kind of want to figure it out."

"You want to buy each other Christmas gifts here...at the airport?" I said hesitantly. Because I was a competitive person, even when it came to gift-giving, and there was no one else I cared about winning the prize for more than the guy excitedly looking around the shop in front of me.

"I do. I really do." He nodded, rubbing his hands together. "Let's find each other's present here at the airport—and it has to be something that can only be found here. No cheating by hitting up the Brooks Brothers or something."

"No Starbucks mug?" I teased, feeling myself getting excited in spite of my better judgment.

"Absolutely not. I want something that looks like you forgot about me and grabbed it at the last minute on your flight home." He started to head to the doorway. "You ready?"

"I'm ready." I bit my lip. Jordan made even being stuck at the airport fun.

He headed out the door, and I spun back around in the store. Where to begin?

"I mean, there's this?" Sarah held up a massive blue mug shaped like the state of Texas. I cringed and headed toward the toiletries.

An hour passed, and I couldn't find anything. I had scoured multiple stores, bumping into Jordan a couple of times, who would wink at me or wiggle his brows, but I came up empty-handed.

"Back to square one?" Jenna asked, who'd been trying to help along the way. We were back in that first shop where we started the game, standing in front of the same magazine rack again. I took in a steadying breath while "Baby, It's Cold Outside" blared through the speakers.

"Back to square one." I shrugged when something caught my eye. It would have to do.

As we settled into our seats on the airplane, Jordan leaned down and whispered against my ear, "Find me a gift?" making my hair stand on end.

I glanced sideways up at him. "I did. You have any luck?"

"I sure did." He smiled smugly as he buckled his seatbelt.

That night, after we'd finally checked into the snow-laden rustic hotel, Jordan and I nestled up by the lobby fireplace under a heavy quilted throw. The wood crackled and the air smelled of pine and ash as Jordan tucked a piece of hair behind my ear.

We'd both brought our presents with us, left in their plastic shopping bags and sitting by our feet. "I don't think I've ever been so excited to exchange presents." Jordan's blue eyes gleamed in the firelight.

I'd caught him trying to peek into the plastic bag all afternoon.

"I don't think you'll ever get another gift quite like this one." I lifted my chin. "There's no competing with the absolute gem I found."

Jordan ran a hand through his hair. "Enough bluffing. Let's see the gift, Soph."

The two of us both grabbed the bags at our feet.

I dropped mine in his lap first. "Open up, buddy."

He pulled the packaging paper off the giant blue Texas-shaped mug and a laugh burst from his lips. "This is heavy," he said pretending he could barely hold it up. "And so beautiful."

I leaned into his arm giggling. "I originally rejected this mug, but it eventually won me over."

Something about Jordan, and how we loved each other, made me feel safe enough to let my competitive stride slow down enough to be silly with him. To stop hunting for perfect and let myself grab hold of whatever made us laugh.

"I will keep this mug forever and always think of the girl who can make me fall in love with just about anything to do with her." He twirled it around his hands, examining it. "This baby is the finest ceramic."

I reached into the plastic bag he'd placed in my lap, grabbing hold of something delicate and small. Dangling from my fingers *was an ornament with a preserved piece of mistletoe in glass, red ribbon tied at its base.*

Tears prickled my eyes. "Jordan, how'd you find this?"

"One of those ornament racks. It was the only one like it. I saw it, and it reminded me—"

"Of our first kiss," I said, breathless. I fingered the ornament. The glass was smooth under my fingertips.

"I owe a lot to mistletoe, you know." He ran his thumb along my jaw. "Still can't believe I get to be the guy kissing you."

"You never did need mistletoe to kiss me," I said, placing my hand against the back of his neck and pulling him in until his lips were firm against mine. He dug his hands into my lower back, pulling me closer. There was nothing as fun as being in love with him.

Years later, I was digging through boxes and tubs as the sun got low in the sky outside the windows until I finally found that ornament of mistletoe encased in glass. Red ribbon looped around my finger as I dangled it in front of me. After all this time, the green leaf of mistletoe was still preserved. The color was unfaded by time and as evergreen as the night by the fire. I ran a finger across it, trying to ignore the thought that when it came to Jordan it sometimes felt my own feelings had been preserved and tucked away all this time, too. And now that we were in the same city, I'd have to pull them out of the box and face just how vibrant and unfaded they may be.

Chapter 3

DECEMBER 31ST, 2022

New Year's Eve night, Orlando and I met Dad and his wife, Heather, at our small town's New Year's Eve Celebration in our bustling downtown. I wore a thick cream sweater dress and a navy knit hat. We arrived to find crowded streets and excitement as thick in the air as the scent of hot chocolate and caramel popcorn. Live music boomed as we weaved through the crowds.

Orlando twirled me to the music until we ran into old friends. Everyone was talking a mile a minute catching up. Dad and Heather bought hot drinks to warm us up. We were swapping stories about silly past Christmas gifts when my eyes landed on someone dancing across the way. I squinted to see Jordan's girlfriend, Emma. Her long blonde hair and bright blue eyes matched the photos of her I'd found on some of his tagged photos online. I searched the faces standing with her for Jordan's, but he wasn't there. She was with the Hernandez siblings. I knew them from school. I pulled my coat tighter around me in the winter night air.

We rushed to the fireworks show as the crowd chanted the countdown. *Five, four.* We found a spot squeezed in the sea of people. *Three, two, one.*

My dad kissed me on the forehead at the stroke of midnight.

"Happy New Year, my girl," he said under fireworks exploding overhead.

I slid an arm around his waist. "Happy new year, Dad," I whispered into his fluffy coat.

"I'm so happy you're home," he said. His voice was nearly lost under the booming fireworks, but I still heard him. Another piece I'd thought was broken and lost forever, safely in my hands again.

"Watch out, Sweet River. Sophie's back this year," Orlando shouted, giving my arm a little nudge. I crinkle my cold, pink nose at him.

Walking back to our car, I quizzed Orlando on his college life back in Austin. When I recognized the big, white Ford F-150 parked in front of our own car, Orlando didn't notice as he climbed into the driver's seat of his Jeep. He was still chattering away unaware who that truck belonged to—since he hadn't been obsessively keeping up with Jordan via social media and mutual friends—but I stayed on the sidewalk for an extra minute, because *what if...*

My eyes landed on Jordan walking toward his truck, looking up at the stars overhead. His eyes took a moment before they settled on me.

He stopped in his tracks as our eyes locked. We hadn't spoken since I broke up with him on his parent's front porch that fall when we were both eighteen. *What's a good icebreaker when you run into your first love?*

"You're back." He spoke first. His voice was rugged, making mist in the air.

I nodded. The fuzzy ball on top of my knit hat bounced with the movement.

"For Christmas?" He kept looking away like it hurt to look at me.

"For good," I said, my heart rocking against my chest. Taking him in after all this time, new creases lined around those same hazel eyes, his sandy locks had grown out a little shaggier, and stubble shadowed his jawline.

His gaze finally locked on mine. "For good?"

"It was time to come home," I said. I'd known I'd probably wind up talking to Jordan eventually, but it still felt so surreal to feel his focus on me again.

"This week just keeps..." His voice trailed off. "You..."

"I..." *Do I apologize for ghosting him after all this time? Do I make a joke? Do I ask him to go grab a coffee and catch up? Do I ask what else happened this week?*

I couldn't shake the image of his swollen eyes on Christmas Eve from my mind, and now, his remark about this week.

"Are you okay?" I asked like a reflex.

He laughed humorlessly, kicking a shoe against the crunchy leaves scattered at our feet. "Not really."

I stepped closer, wanting to find some way to comfort him. "I don't want to add to anything—"

He shook his head, quieting me. "Sophia." His voice saying my name took the air out of my lungs. "It's nothing for you to worry about. You being back home is... *surprising* is all. We can be friends, okay?"

"Okay," I said. I should've felt relief at his words, but instead, it felt like someone snuffing out something I hadn't realized was still burning in my chest.

He opened his driver-side door, then called out, "Welcome back, by the way!"

That night, I tossed and turned, tangled up in my sheets. I hadn't anticipated the memories and feelings talking to Jordan would rustle up. His presence was still a force around me, affecting my gravity. I thought those feelings had been giddy teenage things. Maybe Jordan made me feel like a teenager again at twenty-six? Maybe how Jordan could take up residence in my mind was another one of those things that wouldn't ever change.

I still went back to that October night I broke it off all the time, like tracing an old scar with my fingertips.

While the two of us were on his front porch, Jordan's eyes wrinkled in concern when he answered the door to me and saw my tear-stained cheeks. I was supposed to be hours away at school.

I'd driven all day across the state to talk to him.

He'd consistently been there for me the past few weeks after my parents' divorce, even as I ignored his calls and pulled away. Now, I was here beside him but as far away as could be.

"Sophie," he breathed out after I ended things. The two of us held ourselves against the crisp October air. "Don't do this. Don't do this." He knew I was spinning out of control after the wrecking ball of news about my parents. About my dad and a stranger.

I was desperate to somehow scrape together some new life that didn't hurt so much. Like I could tape something new up over all the pain.

I drove home sobbing with the icy realization that the person I wanted to call right then to comfort me was Jordan. The person I wanted to hold me until I stopped crying was Jordan. The person who knew me well enough to love me through this was Jordan. I'd cut ties with my boyfriend and the best friend I'd ever had in one fell swoop.

But Jordan loved a different me. A me who was dreamy-eyed and hopeful, who thought she'd marry her high school sweetheart.

Two peas in a pod, his mom used to say about us.

Even if he could love this other version of me, and I knew he'd try—Jordan meant trips back home. And home hurt. I didn't think I could handle it.

Classic Sophia, always racing toward the goal, the prize, even when everything screamed to slow down. Always pushing harder and asking for more, even when the prize at the end of the race was a broken heart.

It took a few years for everything I'd taped up over my hurt to fall apart.

My new boyfriend, Tyler, was the perfect distraction. His life as a musician was all-consuming for the both of us. He dropped out of school to pursue his career. Our relationship together consisted mostly of me meeting him on tour stops and in recording studios in between classes. I was more than happy to let both our lives revolve around him. It felt easier than actually dealing with my own needs and wants.

It was strange to go from a relationship where Jordan's love felt so specific to who I was and who he was with me to a relationship where I felt like a supporting role. It felt easier. I could hide away my hurt. I could lick my wounds and cope in whatever unhealthy ways I wanted, and it went unnoticed and unchallenged.

Jordan would've pushed me to call my mom. To check on Orlando. He would've noticed that I cried every time my dad's favorite singer, Thomas Rhett, came on, and he definitely would have asked why I kept playing his songs anyway.

Tyler seemed to think I'd never been close to my family, and I let him believe it. I shared the story of my parents' divorce sparingly like hazardous, dangerous materials.

Our relationship was about him and his music, his family, his fans, his dreams, and I could just float in and out as we pleased. I invested little, barely even my feelings, but reaped affection and distraction.

After college graduation, he asked me to marry him on stage at one of his shows, and it was so loud with the crowd chanting for me to "Say yes, say yes, say yes!"

I said, "Yes," but I wasn't sure he even heard me. He turned to the crowd with a triumphant fist in the air after he slipped the ring on my finger. The applause rang in my ears long after I left the stage.

During our first and only year of marriage, I barely saw him. I finally realized that everything about us was surface and shiny, but not durable, not real. As I peeled the layers back to rediscover myself, Tyler grew more distant. He married a woman I didn't even recognize when I looked in the mirror. He didn't marry me.

As Tyler called to cancel trips back home, over and over, I realized, I didn't know him either. The two of us picked each other like a temporary antidote—me wanting him as a distraction from my real life and him wanting me to bolster his ego when he wasn't on the road.

He didn't even come back to sign the divorce papers or talk to the lawyer. Everything was done from the road. His final goodbye was sent via email and with a heart emoji.

I didn't regret him as much as I regretted running away from my problems, my family, my home, and myself.

In my first year after the divorce, I met with a therapist and admitted aloud, "I loved Sophie from Sweet River, but I ignored her voice for so long I don't know how to recognize it anymore."

She nodded along then said, "Maybe you should start talking to yourself more then? Because Sophia may be in Dallas right now, but she's still the girl from Sweet River."

I spent each week that year re-learning myself in my tiny apartment in Dallas.

Did I still love to run? I hadn't run since high school. I bought myself running clothes, and the first time my feet hit the pavement, my entire body went warm with joy.

Did I miss church? I found a church across town and slipped into the back pew, tears stinging my eyes as we sang an old hymn.

Could I forgive my dad? I'd ignored phone calls and visits for so long. It'd become an old bruise I avoided. Finally, after years, he and his wife drove across the state to spend the weekend with me cooped up in my little apartment overlooking the cityscape. His new wife, Heather, actually made me laugh and taught me how to make cinnamon rolls. Dad was still Dad, I realized, just a lot more imperfect and human than my younger self let herself see. I handled our relationship carefully but made room for him in my life again.

It took a few years, but I found myself again. Sophie from

Sweet River could exist anywhere, I learned, and if I ran away from home, it could still make its way to me.

I was driving back to my apartment from work one day, on the phone with my brother Orlando, when he asked, "If you could live anywhere in the whole world, where would it be?"

It wasn't some tropical island or European city.

My mind immediately went to that old house down the street from Sweet River Elementary. The house Jordan and I would drive by, dreaming of a future together in those walls. I had the words he'd said when they were seventeen memorized like a favorite passage in a book.

I'll fix that house up for you someday. You'll be able to walk to school to teach every morning. Hang twinkle lights at Christmas. We'll paint it any color you want.

My old dreams were still alive, still twinkling like stars that hadn't faded. A heartbroken girl had crushed them in her fist, but an older, smarter version of her was unfurling her hand, sifting through the remnants, reassuring her, "Don't worry, things break. But we can fix them."

DECEMBER 23RD, 2023

My Christmas tree was glowing in the corner of the room as the morning sun streamed through the window blinds. Mom poured me a cup of coffee in the kitchen while she asked, "How are you feeling today? It's a big day."

"It is a big day," I said through an exhale as she placed the mug in my hands. "It's also been a long time coming."

She nodded affirmingly, then glanced down at her watch. "We've got a little time. Want me to pull out the scrapbooks?"

My eyes went wide. I hadn't seen Mom's scrapbooks since we were high schoolers. Not since the divorce. "Yes, please."

I followed her to my bedroom where she'd left her bags. She walked over a canvas tote and slid out an armful of scrapbooks, pulling years' worth of memories from that small tote bag.

"These were once the scary monsters under my bed." She chuckled. "But when I moved into my new house and came across them, it got me pulling them out more."

"Scary as you thought?" I asked as we spread the books out on my bedroom floor, plush gray carpet under us.

Her chin trembled. "Some parts, maybe. But you know what? Mostly they are precious. We made some good memories." She opened the first page to baby pictures. "Little bald baby Orlando."

She turned the page. "That Christmas morning you got your bike. The time Uncle Joe dressed up as Santa." I chuckled at my uncle wearing a big white beard.

I placed my hand on Mom's. I rested my head on her shoulder. "We're filling up more scrapbooks today."

She flipped open one of the books. "There's one I wanted to show you." She turned a few more pages to a page with photos from when Jordan and I had to have been eight or nine. I was dressed up in a pretend wedding dress, a white towel over my head as a veil. Jordan clutched a ring pop in his pocket. His hair was soaked with gel like he'd tried to fix it for the occasion.

I couldn't contain my grin. "I remember this day. We'd made a big deal of this pretend wedding."

"You even got your dad to play the 'Wedding March' on the piano," Mom said through laughter, her finger stroking the picture. "Orlando was your man of honor."

"I guess I knew everything I wanted early on." My eyes filled with tears but in a good way.

Chapter 5

JANUARY 13TH, 2023

Weeks later, after I'd moved into my new place on the same block as my old dream house, I went to visit my dad at work. He owned the auto shop in town. He'd been putting in hours helping me unpack, hang art, and build furniture, so one wintry afternoon, I decided to bring him a warm coffee as a small gesture of thanks.

Snow was on the ground as I scurried through the parking lot. I greeted the receptionist at the front desk so she could let my dad know I was there. I turned away from the desk toward the lobby when Gabriel Hernandez, leaning on a crutch, and Emma,

Jordan's girlfriend, who was suspiciously *never with* Jordan, greeted me. Gabriel was charming as ever with his dark curls and charisma. We started to chat. It was friendly enough, but my mind was screaming at Emma through the small talk, *Are you still dating Jordan? Where is Jordan? Is Jordan single?*

Emma wasn't sharing any updates, anxiously toying with her long blonde hair and laughing along to Gabriel's chatter.

I had to finally bring Jordan up myself. "How are you? *How's Jordan?*" I had an inkling that maybe things had blown up around the time I moved back to town, hence his red-rimmed eyes and puffy cheeks on Christmas Eve.

"I hear he's doing well..." Emma said, and I was about to burst from lack of explanation until bless her, she added, "We're actually just friends now."

I didn't want to say I was happy or ecstatic, but I was relieved —and maybe a reckless kind of hopeful. The conversation was a blur after that, ending shortly after, but its effect on me lingered.

My mind reeled... *Jordan was single*. What did that mean? Did that mean anything at all? Was it allowed to mean something to me?

I left Dad's shop in the afternoon, snow coming down thick like fog while I drove home. As I turned onto my block, my heart tugged in my chest until I drove straight past my new place, not stopping until I arrived in front of that old dream house down the street where all my old dreams still lived. I hadn't forced myself to box them up and carry them out yet. *Maybe someday the house could still be mine? No one else had claimed it yet.*

Putting my Corolla into park, I recognized the white truck parked in front of the house across from me.

The truck's engine was loudly running. I squinted and saw Jordan laughing in his front seat. My chin dipped down. *Oh, so funny, Jordan catching me revisiting our old spots.*

I unbuckled and stepped out of my car with him stepping out of his at the same time.

He rubbed his hands together in the cold. "Fancy meeting you here?" he said. His sandy hair was messy like he'd tousled it before sliding out of his truck.

"I live down the street now in one of those townhouses across the park." I gestured behind me as if that explained my presence here. Snow crunched under my boots.

"Remember how we used to come here all the time as teenagers? We'd dream about the future and talk for hours. I guess I never stopped. I still come by here to think," he said. "Is that weird?"

"No, not weird at all. I was planning to come here to think, myself." *If I was still coming back to our old spots, at least he was, too.* Snow landed on my hair and my clothes. He dusted it off his coat.

I gave a little shiver, the cold seeping through my puffy white coat.

"Truck Chat?" he asked.

Truck Chats, our old term for long talks we'd have in his truck. It was a different truck back then than this fancy new model I was currently climbing into. But the term still filled my chest with a familiar warmth.

A fight? We needed a Truck Chat. Just watched a good movie we needed to dissect. Truck Chat. Stressed about school? Truck Chat. Planning the holidays? Truck Chat. Needed a pep talk? Truck Chat.

"I've been long overdue for a Truck Chat," I said, relaxing into his front seat. I was hit with the familiar piney, spicy scent I'd always known as Jordan's. A scent that still showed up in my dreams.

Here he sat blood spikingly close, his breath fogging up the window shield, grinning at me like we were old friends, smelling like my teenage dreams. A Truck Chat, like no time had passed.

"How's it being back in town?" he asked, waking me from my thoughts.

"It's been exactly what I needed." I warmed my hands with the truck heaters. "I've been eating at all my favorite spots.

Catching up with everyone. It's pretty wonderful how Sweet River welcomed me back like no time has passed."

"Eh, in the grand scheme of things, you were here longer than you weren't." Jordan shrugged, still able to shrink my fears in one sentence.

"Sometimes, it feels like my time away was mostly me piecing myself back together." I sighed.

"I can't imagine you being anything but that bold Sophia I always knew," he said. "I know how hard things were for you, though. It must've taken time."

"It took a few years, but I did some growing that makes me proud. It just felt like I needed to get away from everything to do it."

"You needed to be repotted for a bit?" Jordan nodded. His five o'clock shadow was sharper than I'd ever seen it.

"Sure. Now, I'm ready to dig my roots into Sweet River soil again." I peeked out the window to the ripple of gray overhead.

We hadn't spoken like this in years. My heart was a humming-bird in my chest. Jordan cleared his throat.

"I've got to ask." His voice was low. "What brought you back to our Sweet River soil?"

"I finally stopped fearing how badly I wanted to come home." It was honest, maybe too honest, but this was a Truck Chat, wasn't it?

"Scared of little old Sweet River?" Jordan said in mock surprise. "Summer festivals and coffee shops and—" I crossed the console and gave him a shove. "There's a whole lotta history here, I know."

"I missed these chats," I admitted. *I missed you.*

"We spent a lot of time in that old truck of mine," he said distantly like his mind was far away in a memory.

I swallowed back my visceral reaction to the memory of how we used to tangle up in the back of his truck and kiss across consoles. "Uh-huh," I murmured, my skin suddenly warmer.

"Remember that long drive to Galveston?"

"Yes. I said I wanted to watch the sunrise over the beach some-day." I played with the zipper on my coat. "So you decided to drive me to the beach the very next morning."

"You were not happy about that wake-up call." He was grinning wide and boyish.

"Well, you did come knocking at my window at three a.m."

"I thought you'd tell me to go home, honestly."

"I wasn't going to ever turn you away," I said through a lump in my throat.

I could still hear us laughing groggy and giddy as we drove along the darkened highways. Playing twenty questions to stay awake, singing country music to each other, his Tim McGraw to my Faith Hill.

I could still feel our sandy feet in the cold morning sand, watching the sun come up over the bay in pink blush and turquoise.

Jordan was playful and giddy as he made my dreams come true. "You know, Rogers," his favorite nickname for me, the one that felt like a comforting kiss on the forehead every time he said it. "I'm just so happy to have you here in my arms," he'd said, my back against his chest, his arms encircling me, my fortress of forearms and warm skin.

"It was a sad day when I had to turn that truck in," Jordan said finally, his head hanging low. "I needed a bigger, newer model when I started the business."

"I've seen that ad for your home construction business all over town since I got back," I said admiringly. A picture of him and his dad with tool belts on was slapped on nearly every bus and store window.

"You can't escape me, huh?" he joked, but he had no idea how true it was. Jordan was around every corner, ads or not. And, even when he wasn't, here I was driving down the street to revisit our memories.

"I take it work is good?" I asked.

"Yeah, yeah. It's fun," he said, his eyes looking nearly gold today. I knew how bad he'd wanted it. "You get hired at Sweet River Elementary?"

"I did. I took over for someone who left on maternity leave in January. A sweet class of second graders," I said, then chuckled. "There are a couple of, uh, unruly kiddos. But there always are."

He smiled. "I can picture you tussling with 'em."

"You know I can tussle," I said, chin up.

"Oh, I know. I remember you out there during flag football taking on the big boys."

"Or how I'd always beat you on the track." I couldn't help bringing it up. Crimson flush spread from his cheeks to his ears, the way it always did.

He shook his head. "There's the Sophie smack talk." *Sophie*. It was probably an accidental slip but hearing him say it felt like winning a medal.

"What some call smack talk, others call truth," I said. A car drove past us, slow on the snowy street. "How's..." *Could I ask about Emma? His love life?*

He narrowed his eyes, reading me like a favorite book. "You're feeling nosey, I see?"

"Always." I gave a big smile.

"That question requires a little liquid assistance." He reached for his bag. I raised a brow as he pulled out a thermos. *Oh, I knew that thermos.*

"Your nana is still sending you off with hot cocoa on cold days?" I laughed. "You're twenty-six—nearly thirty."

"Only on the days I stop by to bring her lunch or take her to her nail appointments. She's not driving anymore, you know." He poured a little cocoa into the lid that also doubled as a cup. He took a sip before offering me one.

Steamy milk chocolate with the perfect hint of peppermint warmed me down to my toes. "Still the best," I said after taking a sip.

He held the lid in his hands as he said, "Emma and I ended it back in December. Right before Christmas." *Definitely the reason for the sad Christmas caroling.*

"How long had you two been...a thing?" I asked, trying to keep the emotion out of my voice. It wasn't fair for me to feel jealous, but feelings never do play by the rules.

"We'd been together for a couple of years," he said. "*Not eight years.* But not nothing."

"I'm also single," I offered. "My breakup had been a long time coming, though. Doomed from the start, some may say."

"Mine was a long time coming, too, I think. I was trying to ignore the signs, thinking I could force it into what I wanted," he said quietly, reflectively. "I think she felt like I was trying to make her into someone she wasn't."

"Who?" I asked. The word out before I could remember to hold it back. I never could hold anything back with him.

He grinned like I already knew the answer. "The girl my dreams come true with. Who wants what I want. Old house, noisy kids, and weekend mornings with syrup and pancakes."

"Who wouldn't want those things?"

"She didn't." He tapped the thermos thoughtfully. "You didn't."

I let out a breath like I'd just been punched in the throat. *It wasn't that simple.*

"I'll be okay. I can survive this fender bender of a breakup after the way my heart was totaled after the car crash of us," he said this plainly like it was just the facts. As if my eyes weren't filling with tears.

I blinked them away and looked out the window. "I'm sorry." Which heartbreak was I sorry for?

He put his eyes on mine and said, "Thank you. Really." He looked out the windshield thoughtfully. "It's all taught stubbornly hopeful me that I've got to be patient and wait for the right person. The one where our dreams and our desires line up. I can't force it from sheer force of *want*. When it's right, it'll be natural."

I wasn't sure what I was allowed to be feeling in this moment —I'd been the one who totaled his heart. Someone who'd taught him that he might want our lives to align, but that desire alone couldn't make it so.

But what if they aligned now? We were both still parked outside the same dream house, weren't we?

"Just 'cause I want someone to be the one, doesn't mean she is, right?"

"Right," I said it so softly, I wasn't sure he even heard me.

Later that night, I tore into the cardboard box where I kept my most valuable mementos and artifacts. Sorting through the old postcards from my grandparents and ticket stubs from trips, until my fingers touched the letter I'd read so many times I knew it by heart. It was the letter Jordan sent the autumn of our breakup. It was water stained from my own tear drops.

Dear Sophia,

You drove off a few days ago. It honestly feels like you took my heart right out of my chest with you. I was praying this morning at church and said to God, "It feels like everything is falling apart." Then, I thought, what I'm feeling can't compare to how you're feeling. Everything for you really is falling apart.

I know how badly your dad hurt you. You asked me if I think he regretted your family since he fell in love with someone else, and there's no way, Sophie. I know your dad is obsessed with you and Orlando. But I'm not the one to ask. He's got your answer. Call him and ask him that. Or call him and yell at him.

Or call Orlando and talk about it. Come back and see your mom. Don't shove it all away.

I know you, Sophie, you want to race toward the goal, and your goal right now is to avoid the hurt. I know it hurts, but I've seen you over the years. You're strong enough to handle it.

Maybe you're right and handling it without our relationship distracting you will make it easier. I hope so. But if you realize you need my help. Or you change your mind. I hope you remember that I'm always here for you, Rogers.

I'm so sorry about your parents. I saw the movers at your house yesterday, and it made me break down in tears. All our memories making dinner in your kitchen with your mom or when we were kids playing hide and seek in your backyard. It kills me. I've enclosed a few leaves from the oak tree in your backyard since I know you won't have time to say bye yourself.

I know how much you have on your shoulders right now, and if our relationship feels like any added weight, I understand. I'll be whatever you need, even if that's just a happy old memory.

Love you forever,
Jordan

Chapter 6

DECEMBER 23RD, 2023

Mom and I finally put the scrapbooks away so I could get started on the morning of preparation ahead of me. The first thing on my to-do list was a shower.

I was still trying to steady myself—nothing about today felt real. It felt like I was walking around in a snowy dream.

This is real, I repeated to myself. *Enjoy it.* I opened my hands to the hot water prickling my skin while steam and eucalyptus filled my senses. I lathered up a loofah of bubbly soap, brushing it against the moon-shaped scar on my knee that had never fully faded. I couldn't see that scar without smiling. I wore it like a tattoo ode to Jordan. I ran my finger over the raised skin, and it took me right back to the memory.

I had taken running seriously since I was four years old, always keeping up with the boys, and always up for the challenge of a race. Jordan and the other neighborhood kids would show up on my doorstep and call for me to come play, and I'd race out full speed.

This only got stronger with age. Jordan, my best friend, always tagged along. He was one of the best runners—with a natural budding athleticism that everyone could see even at eight years old. That didn't scare me, though. It made me go faster.

One December, when we were both twelve years old, the two of us were in a kid's race for a local charity to buy Christmas presents for the children's hospital. Jordan and I were taking the lead, side by side. Sneakers thudding against gravel. The cold sting of a chilly winter morning. Rhythmic breathing as I steadied my pace.

My mind was on the prize: the winner of the race always got a photo on the front page of the Sweet River Gazette, a special medal, and a giant candy package of my eight-year-old sugar plum dreams. Jordan and I had been arguing over who would win since it was our first year old enough to race. I'd been imagining every piece of delicious Christmas candy in that winner's basket with my mouth watering.

Now here he was, taking the lead, with bright red fuzzy antlers on his head that jingled with his every stride.

I tried to push myself further when my sneaker hit the path the wrong way and *bam!* I hit the ground knee first. I grabbed my knee in pain, but also shame, as Mom called out my name from the sidelines and other kids passed right by me.

No. No. Not now. My eyes were squeezed tight, shocked little tears pooled in my eyes as I lay there on the pavement.

I felt his warmth hovering nearby before I opened my eyes to see him. "Take a tumble, Sophie?" he asked, trying to make light of my predicament. I appreciated it more than he knew.

"Just a small one," I whispered, trying not to cry as he knelt down beside me.

"It's your knee?" he asked, reaching for it, gently wiping away the smear of blood. He helped me wobble to my feet, the two of us realizing with relief that it wasn't a serious injury. Jordan swooped me into his gangly pre-teen arms and carried me across the finish line. My stomach filled with butterflies because to me he was a knight in shiny sneakers—and antlers.

Neither of us won. But I knew Jordan could've won.

He could've crossed the finish line, then come back for me. He could've been so focused on the goal that he didn't notice if I fell or not. A different person might've assumed I was fine and kept going after a quick, *Are you okay?*

But Jordan always noticed me even if he was steps ahead.

At a victory breakfast with our families, everyone cheered as he called us, "The two fastest losers of the race." He laughed when he said it, and I could practically feel the hearts springing out of my eyes as I watched him.

He'd made me fall in love with him a little bit right there on the running path.

Chapter 7

JANUARY 22ND, 2023

ORLANDO

SOPH. You need to get out of your house. I'm thinking I'll come down to Sweet River for the weekend and invite some of our friends in town to skate.

ME

Skating?

ORLANDO

Yeah, City Hall leaves the rink up until Feb!

ME

I mean skating? as in, are we sure about this being the chosen activity?

ORLANDO

You fell one time, Soph

Orlando was worried about me. He was worried I was lonely coming back to town—even after I assured him I was making friends at the school and reconnecting with people from my past. He drove to Sweet River for the weekend and invited some of his local friends and our old mutual friend group to meet at the winter skate rink in front of Sweet River City Hall.

But I hate skating, I grumbled to myself that Saturday morning as I hung onto the sides of the rink for dear life. It was cute, this ice rink with fluffy green garland lining the sides and twinkle lights hanging overhead. Christmas trees were still glowing by the sidewalks. A big fake snowman with a mittened hand waved at the entrance.

But I still hated skating. I sniffled in the cold, latching onto Orlando as he skated by. The creamy scent of hot chocolate and sugary marshmallows wafted from the hot cocoa stand.

"Sophia, why don't you ask if they have those kids' stabilizers in a bigger size?" Orlando offered, slowing down for me.

"I have my pride, Orlando," I whispered. "I am not asking for that. Can you be my stabilizer, please?"

He sighed as if I was really putting him out. A few of our friends started calling over, urging us to speed up, but I yanked him closer with a death grip when he tried to change our pace.

"Soph, are you new to skating?" Jeremy, Orlando's best friend since toddler years, asked as he skated up.

"No, I've skated before," I said, my fluffy coat bumping into Orlando's.

"She's just terrible," Orlando offered, laughing when I widened my eyes at him.

"I'm nervous, okay? I've had some bad falls—"

"Bad falls?" Orlando said aghast. "She fell once when she was a kid, and I caught her!"

"You were a tiny twig so that fall still hurt." I pulled him to a stop. The three of us huddled on the ice.

"I can help you out. *I don't mind taking it slow*," Jeremy said, and there was a certain twinkle in his eyes that made me wonder if he meant something more than skating.

I swallowed.

"Great idea. Jeremy, you're a saint." Orlando patted his friend on the back and skated off to our friend Anna who he'd been watching from across the rink.

I gave Jeremy a nervous smile as he looped his arm in mine. Jeremy had always been my younger brother's silly sidekick, and I didn't want to give him any ideas.

"How's it being back in town?" he asked, tugging on his beanie. The air was frigid today.

"It's been really nice. Everyone has been really welcoming, you know? It's fun to see what shops have changed and what restaurants are new, like the Tavern downtown. And I've seen some people I didn't realize how badly I missed, like old teachers and friends I hadn't seen in forever." Our pace was slow as molasses. I could feel my nose turning pink.

"Did you miss me?" Jeremy joked, dramatically slapping his hand to his chest. I wasn't even sure I'd classify this as flirting since Jeremy had always been like this.

I opened my mouth to answer when I noticed Jordan standing across from us at the hot cocoa stand. His gaze was on Jeremy and me.

"Well?" Jeremy gave my arm a light squeeze.

"Uh, yeah, totally," I said mindlessly, taking in Jordan's expression, our eyes locking for a moment before he looked away. Tight jaw, steely eyes. I knew that look. It was the same one he had back when we were sixteen and my lab partner, Ben, wrote me a note confessing his longtime crush.

Jordan was jealous. A thrill shot through my spine. I didn't want him feeling bad, but maybe, just maybe, in some way, I still affected him like he did me.

"Well, I've got to say, I know your brother sure is happy to have you home. He was pumped to put this skate meet-up together for you to make sure you're happy enough here so you don't run off again." Jeremy was laughing like it was ridiculous of him, but it tugged on my heartstrings.

"I'm not running off anywhere," I said, glancing sideways at him. "You can tell him I said that."

"I'll tell him. You can, too," Jeremy said, then slid us to a stop by the rink exit. "I don't know about you, but I am freezing. Want me to grab us some hot chocolate or coffee?"

Jordan was steps away from us in line. He shot a backward glance our way. My stomach swooped in a way it hadn't in forever. *It felt good.*

"Coffee sounds great," I said.

"I'll leave you here." Jeremy helped me off the ice and onto a bench on the sidelines. "But I promise I'll be right back." He meant it jokingly, but my eyes were on Jordan. I saw him shake his head.

"If I fall and break something while you're gone, it's on you," I teased, making Jeremy laugh as he shuffled in his skates into the waiting line.

I started to unstrap my skates while Jordan moved to the side of the stand to wait for his order to be made. Discreetly, I glanced around the rink to see if I could spot who was with him.

"Hey, Soph, how do you like your coffee?" Jeremy called from his spot at the register, over the sound of squealing kids and giggling teenagers.

"Um." I tried to think for a moment.

"She likes a medium, hot, with a splash of cream and cinnamon drizzled on top," Jordan said his voice low like this was a reflex he didn't want but couldn't help. His gaze met mine as he added, "A big splash of cream, actually."

Jeremy let his eyes follow from Jordan to me. He knew our history. He'd witnessed it firsthand at birthday parties and football games over the years. He raised a brow to me in question.

I nodded, my mouth dry. "He's right. That's exactly how I like it."

Jeremy turned and repeated the order to the barista. I stood up, walking a few steps closer to the stand, closer to Jordan.

"You remember?" My voice was quiet as falling snow.

Jordan looked at me with half a smile and sad eyes. "Used to be more important to me that I got your order right than my own."

"Used to be," I said. I remembered that feeling deep in my bones. A frosty breeze blew my hair across my eyes.

He looked down at his feet. "Used to be."

FEBRUARY 2ND, 2023

> Hey guys, I'm here and grabbed us a bench for whoever can make it to the game tonight! It's the third row.
>
> also there's a discount on popcorn for the staff—make sure to show your badge

CAROLINE

> It's Mr. Ritchie's son who's in charge tonight and he has a heavy hand with the butter, so you'll wanna grab some

One of my favorite things about living in a small town in Texas was the high school sports games. The crowds were loud and full, the snacks were relished more than any five-star dining situation, gossip was made and shared in the span of a few hours, and you never knew who you might run into.

Or find yourself sitting by.

I'd donned my oversized gray Sweet River High sweatshirt for the basketball game that early February night. I strolled inside hit by waves of nostalgia and the scent of nacho cheese. I got myself a tub of popcorn and a soda and made my way into the gym, squinting into the bleachers to find Diane, our art teacher, pointing to the empty spot beside her. I squeezed through the stands toward her and our small teacher group.

I plopped down beside them.

Before I could say hello, I heard a familiar deep voice rumble, "I like the sweatshirt."

In shock, I jerked to the right, popcorn flinging from my tub as I startled, to find two warm hazel eyes on me. *Jordan*.

Jordan was currently covered in my freshly buttered popcorn. It was a tragedy on so many levels.

I had been zeroed in on finding Diane and our teacher crew. I hadn't noticed one of the most important faces in my life sitting beside them.

"Oh no. Oh no," I repeated, scrambling to pick kernels off his navy sweater, feeling my face flush. "I didn't mean to spill this on you!"

"You mean you didn't mean to throw popcorn as some evil act of vengeance for how I used to crush you on the court?" He was smiling down at me as I dusted salt off his torturously broad chest. A smile I knew well, the one when he pitied me and found me cute at the same time.

I immediately pulled back. *"Crushed me on the court? Dream on."*

He chuckled. Sneakers squeaked across the court below.

I spotted a few more kernels on his jeans, saying, "I am sorry." I buried my face in my salty hands.

He leaned in closer, peering into the half-empty tub in my lap. "You know, sharing that last half would more than make up for it? Throw in some nachos, and honestly, I'll be glad you spilled on me."

"Deal." I reached out a hand, and we shook on it, defenses between us melting like butter.

Jordan and I came back from the concessions with more

popcorn, two pickles, an order of nachos, and a large soda for Jordan. As we settled back into our seats, Jordan had already finished his pickle and was gulping down his soda. I'd forgotten how much he ate. I used to say he had to fuel all his motion. Always running, always playing a game, building something new, throwing a ball, talking to a neighbor.

"How's the new apartment coming along?" Jordan woke me from my thoughts like we were old pals and checked in on each other.

"It's coming along nicely," I said, then after taking a sip of my soda continued. "Pictures have been hung. Furniture arranged. I have this perfect view from my living room and bedroom of the park across the street."

"Oh, yeah, Hall Park?" Jordan said, and I nodded. "I've coached kids' soccer there the past few years."

"Why does the sound of you coaching soccer on the weekend make perfect sense?" The shot clock buzzed. People shouted around us.

"I started for my nephew, and I guess it stuck."

"You have multiple nieces and nephews now, right?" I asked as if I hadn't been following along the past few years through social media and conversations with mutual friends.

"Two nephews and two nieces. It's the best." He opened his phone and started swiping through photos, leaning close to show me. Him holding tiny, pink babies. Him with a little toddler girl on his shoulders.

"That's Kimber," he said her name softly. Him at the zoo making funny faces with two little boys in front of the monkeys. "Those two can wreak havoc, but they're hilarious."

"This one," I pointed at the sandy-haired one with a wide smile. "Looks like you."

Jordan gazed lovingly at the photo. "You think?"

"Spitting image of you as a boy," I said, taking in Jordan's own sandy hair and big smile.

"That's Logan," he said. "He is actually severely hard of hearing. He's not deaf, but we realized when he was barely a toddler, he was having trouble hearing. He just got cochlear implants. It's been a lot on Jenna." He softened as he said his sister's name. "She's a mom now. It's crazy. And she's a really good one."

"I'm sure she is a good one," I said over the noise of the crowd around us. Jenna was always so strong and steady, keeping us younger kids in check. It was easy to imagine her as a mom now.

"It's been fun to watch." He closed his phone. "Is it weird? You left, and I was just this dumb nineteen-year-old kid. You come back, and I'm an uncle with a bigger family."

"Your family has always been giant." I popped a piece of popcorn in my mouth. "You all keep growing and growing. Soon you'll take over Sweet River."

He leaned back against the stands. "How's Orlando?"

"He's in college now. We keep going in circles around his major. He's not sure what he wants to do when he 'grows up.'" I had to fight the physical urge to lean into Jordan or interlace my fingers with his as we spoke, like some agonizing muscle memory.

"Grown-up Orlando." Jordan shook his head at the thought.

The conversation kept unrolling like an endless path before us. We had so much to catch up on. I glanced toward my teacher friends who were immersed in a group conversation I hadn't even noticed. Jordan and I were in our own bubble.

Jordan was telling me about his grandmother's health, and I was telling him about how my dad and I started talking again. I made eye contact with Diane, who wiggled her eyebrows at me. I knew later she and the whole group would want to know every-thing about the guy who stole my attention at the game.

Growing up, these high school games felt long and eventful. So much could happen on the court and in the stands, and some-times I'd want it to wrap up so I could go home.

Not tonight. Before I was ready...there was the final buzzer, everyone standing to their feet and packing up. Jordan and I cut off mid-conversation. He shrugged. His friends turned to him to discuss their plans for the rest of the night—me, not included.

"Who's the guy?" Diane whispered to me as I gathered my empty popcorn tub and soda cup. Diane hadn't grown up in Sweet River like half of the other teachers on staff.

"An old..." *Friend? Flame?* Nothing about my feelings for Jordan felt old right now. If anything, they felt new after all this time. A seed planted long ago, after all this time still growing. *Ex*, I finally mouthed. Her eyes widened.

But he was so much more than that.

The group of teachers around me invited me to grab food downtown. Thankfully, they'd become a warm welcoming friend group for me the past couple months. I was half-listening, my eyes on Jordan as he and his friends started to exit the stands.

I hadn't realized how much I'd wanted this time with him until I was watching it slip away like water through my fingers.

I probably shouldn't be blatantly staring at him like this, I chastised myself ineffectively.

He stepped onto the gym floor, then turned and looked up into the stands. His smile widened as his eyes landed on me. He raised a hand in a lazy wave like he'd always done.

The dose of nostalgia, of this man in this school beaming up at me, was like waves at high tide. I felt breathless from the impact.

I could almost hear his voice from a decade ago yelling out, *See you, Sophie!* and I'd say back, *Not if I see you first*, and our friends would roll their eyes at our cheesy, high school romance.

I raised my hand, too, and gave a small wave. He paused. His smile fell but not in an unhappy way. Instead, it looked like maybe the memory was pulling him under, too. His friend patted him on the shoulder, and he turned to follow them out the door.

I'd known seeing Jordan again was going to ache a little. Letting him go was a hasty, desperate choice from my young adult years. I'd moved on, so it was an ache I was prepared to ignore. But what I was feeling right now was so much stronger than an ache in the background. These feelings were burning in my chest.

Chapter 9

FEBRUARY 4TH, 2023

I found out Jordan's grandmother had passed on a Saturday morning. My mom had called while I was sleepily rummaging around in my kitchen, so I put her on speaker and placed my phone on the kitchen island. My feet were cold on the kitchen tile while I poured myself a cup of coffee.

Her opening line, "Did you hear the news?"

"What news?" I yawned, bringing my mug toward my lips.

"Jordan's nana died, hon." Her voice was urgent, echoing through my kitchen.

I stood frozen in place. She kept talking, filling the room with the details of what had happened, what she'd heard. I appreciated it, but all I wanted right then was to hear *Jordan's voice*. Hear *his* details.

I wasn't thinking clearly. I didn't even hang up with my mother. I ran to my bedroom, then clumsily yanked on the first pair of yoga pants I saw, an oversized cable knit sweater, some Ugg boots, and a beanie.

"Mom," I yelled. "I've got to go!" I grabbed my purse, slid my finger over the phone screen to end the call, and ran out the door.

. . .

It didn't occur to me until I was walking up his family's driveway that my presence might not be welcome. Or wanted. Or warranted.

I was not a significant person to Jordan anymore. Not his caretaker or honorary family member. I wasn't the one who stood by his side at the funeral.

I hadn't even spoken with his family in eight years.

What am I doing? Classic Sophia running ahead without stopping to think. All action, no plan.

I started to back down the slick sidewalk, the sky a stormy gray. I'd forgotten a coat and my skin felt raw in the winter cold. I walked back to my car, reaching for the keys I'd dropped in my purse seconds before but couldn't find them.

How could I have lost my keys in mere seconds? I stood outside my car digging in my purse.

"Sophia?" Said a light, soft voice I knew as well as my own mother's. I turned to find Jordan's mom, Pat. "You came," she said, like it was a good thing, a right choice. She walked toward me, arms open and pulled me tight against her.

"Of course, I did." My voice was wobbly.

She leaned out of the hug an inch to look at my face. Her hazel eyes were the same as Jordan's but with a few new laugh lines. "Jordan's a mess. We're all a mess. What are we... Well, we weren't ready."

I shook my head. "I'm so sorry." Then I realized I'd shown up empty-handed. No meal or flowers. "Oh, my arms are empty. I didn't bring—"

"No, no, your arms are full already." She squeezed my shoulders in our embrace. "They'll be full all day. I was about to leave to run an errand, but come in."

She led me up the front steps under their big white covered porch. She pushed open a red door that I'd helped paint in elementary school.

The entryway was airy and open, leading into the living room.

The house was full of people as I walked inside, the smell of baked goods and flowers filled the air. I glanced around the house, through the open space living room that spread into the kitchen... until I spotted him.

Jordan was leaning against the kitchen bar talking with his sister. Gray sweatpants and wool socks, bed head. Like he'd found out and came straight to his parent's place. I'd known exactly where to find him.

"Jordan," I said. My voice was tight as I bridged the gap between us. He stopped his conversation when he heard my voice, immediately standing straight and looking for me. When his eyes hooked into mine, something between us crumbled.

"Sophie." His voice cracked as he made his way toward me.

"Jordan," I said again, wrapping my arms around him. His height required him to lean down into me. He held me so close I was pulled onto my toes. The embrace was tight, warm, needy. I rubbed his back the way I knew he found comforting. He buried his head in my dark hair, hot breath against my neck.

Minutes passed. People talked around us. The doorbell rang. Their old family dog came and sniffed my shoes and left, but we stayed embraced. When we pulled apart, I stumbled on my feet.

"I didn't even have to..." His voice trailed off.

"I rushed over the minute I heard the news. I didn't even think twice..." *Didn't even stop to brush my hair.* "Jordan, I'm so sorry."

He took in a jagged breath. "She had a full life. A good one, too. I just think we all..."

"You all feel what you feel," I offered.

He sighed and his shoulders relaxed as he said, "Yeah, that."

Jordan wrapped his hand around my wrist and led me through the living room into the kitchen where his sisters, brother, and dad were standing around lost in conversation, eyes downcast.

"Sophia's here," Jordan said gently, somewhere between an announcement and a heads-up.

His sisters both jerked their heads up.

Jenna's mouth fell open slightly, before she said, "Well, hi."

"It's been a while," Sarah, his sister, added, crossing her arms over her chest.

"I know—" I started.

"She's only been back in town for a couple months," Jordan said, his voice strong as armor.

"It means a lot you'd come over here, even after all this time." Carson, his dad, crossed the kitchen to wrap me up in a bear hug.

"You were one of Nana's favorite people. After you, um, left town, I don't think she ever stopped telling stories about you. Like the time you got out there and beat all of us boy cousins at flag football," Cody, his brother, threw in from his spot slouched against the marbled kitchen counter. Jordan's dad pulled out of our hug, standing beside me in front of the sink.

"Nothing Nana loved more than seeing someone put me in my place," Jordan said with a halfhearted chuckle.

"Nothing she loved more than her grandkids," I said.

"She was our biggest cheerleader one minute then picking on us the next," Jenna said quietly, still not looking at me.

It was awkward timing for me to show up, but also, the most necessary timing. While his sisters weren't making eye contact, Jordan kept looking at me like a life raft.

"I'm so sorry, you guys," I said, trying to keep the trembling out of my voice.

"Thanks, Sophia," Cody and Carson said in unison. Sarah nodded at me.

"Thanks," Jenna said. I reached out to her and gave her hand a small squeeze.

I wasn't here for me, or my past, or my feelings. I was here to help, so I got swept up into the rhythm of the home. I made tea, stored the casseroles dropped at the door, hugged hunched shoulders and listened to tearful voices, helped start a fire in the fireplace, and washed dishes.

The day was winding to a close, everyone sitting around the

living room with a fire crackling in the hearth, family and close friends slowly taking leave. I knew my turn to head out the door was ticking closer.

"What about you, Sophie?" Jordan asked. The family had been sharing funny quirks they loved about Nana Silk.

Everyone's eyes landed expectantly on me. I knew immediately my favorite quirk.

"Her locket," I said, mindlessly touching my own bare neck. "She wore that gold locket with Herb's picture in it every single day since I was a little girl. She'd even let me wear it sometimes." I remembered looking in the mirror when she did and how she'd say I looked so beautiful and grown up.

"She never took it off," Sarah mused.

I was nestled in beside Jordan, close as we could be without blurring the lines. He reached his warm hand toward mine and lightly rubbed the thin skin of my knuckles with his rough fingertips. My whole body flooded with warmth. I lifted my eyes to him, but he was looking at the fire, thinking.

It was my turn to go, but I didn't want to leave.

In the days between my visit and the funeral, I'd gone back to work, but Jordan and I had taken to text messages and phone calls. As if this had somehow built back a bridge of our old relationship, even if now as old friends.

I wore a snug knit black midi dress, black pumps, and my hair loose around my shoulders the day of the funeral. I knew I wasn't a girlfriend, not even his most recent ex, so I'd found a pew in the back as I waited for my mom to arrive. I was going to respectfully hang back.

But, Jordan, who'd been standing at the front of the church, noticed me and walked right over. His big quarterback body was framed in a dark suit.

"Ma'am, why are you way back here?" he said, his voice low, just for us.

"I'm waiting for my mom," I offered, feebly.

"Is Orlando coming?" I knew him, he wanted to confirm she wouldn't be left alone if he whisked me away.

I nodded.

He looped his hand with mine and pulled me from my seat. We laced our fingers together as he led me to his family's row. His rough fingers and warm palm felt as right as they ever did.

Jordan's hand stayed in mine through the entire service, the receiving line, and then back home for the reception at his aunt's house. Holding on tight like somehow my touch was a remedy.

Lines could be blurry. I didn't care and held his hand right back.

When the day came to an end, we were standing outside his aunt's house beside my car on the country road, tall pecan trees blowing in the wind, gravel road underfoot. My back was against the car door, his two arms resting on the roof of the car over my head. My face was basically in his chest. I took a deep breath of his spicy, piney scent.

"Thank you for being here. You didn't have to be. I didn't even ask. You...*showed up*. Both times," he said.

"I wanted to be here," I said soft as a touch.

"How is it, Sophie, no matter the situation, the problem... you're always the fix?" he asked, his southern accent rough against the words.

"It's not me," I said because it wasn't—it was *us*. Together, *we* were the fix. But this wasn't the time to say that to him. I wasn't even sure there was a right time to tell him about the confusing things I felt.

"For me, you always are." He brought his forehead against mine, and my whole body felt warm, dizzy. I closed my eyes. "I couldn't have made it today without you."

"You could've. You've always been so strong for me when I needed it. Like this unwavering force in my life," I said, our foreheads still touching. "But I'm grateful when you were low, I could help hold you up, too."

"I know I'll get through it. It just stings right now. I keep having memories of Nana hit me out of the blue." He pulled us apart, barely an inch, his teary eyes focused on me.

"You know what I've learned? At first, memories feel like poison. But sometimes, they can actually be a balm. They can heal the hurt, soften the pain," I said, slipping my arms around his neck, as he brought his big hands down from the car and wrapped them around my waist.

"I still can't believe you came back home," he whispered into my hair as we tightened our embrace. He was holding me, but there was still a hesitancy between us.

"Back home for good," I said it like a promise.

It was hard to let go. To put myself in my car. To hit the gas as he stood in the driveway, head hanging low. I cried the whole way home.

Chapter 10

FEBRUARY 14TH, 2023

GALENTINES DINNER XOXO
LUCY RHODES

Hi my beautiful Galentines! Just a reminder for tonight—we're meeting at the restaurant at 6:15! I can't wait to see all of you! So grateful to call each of you friend <3

A little over a week passed, and I didn't hear much from Jordan. It was a loaded quiet between us, tense like a held breath. Had those days with texting and touching been a grief-ridden lapse in his judgment? Old flames still flickering?

Or was he just busy?

Or, maybe, like me, he didn't know what we were supposed to say now? I'd sent him a message checking in, and he'd responded kindly but shortly. After we'd held hands and held each other, it still felt blurry between us, like snow on the windshield.

Valentine's Day rolled around, and I woke up to rain thudding against my window, so I spent the morning planning a craft for school next week and watching Julia Roberts run away from a wedding on my TV screen. I wanted to think of anything except Jordan.

A few of my fellow teachers invited me to go to a Valentine's Dinner with them at an Italian restaurant downtown, and weeks ago, I had halfheartedly agreed to go. But then Lucy Rhodes, a bubbly kindergarten teacher, created a group thread titled "Galentines Dinner" with the four teachers in it, so it made bailing even more awkward.

As the group thread lit up, I sighed with the realization I wasn't getting out of this dinner.

I wore a soft pink sweater and my best-fitting jeans and added a few curls to my dark waves before heading out.

Red heart-shaped balloons dangled from the ceiling, candles flickered in the middle of each table, and my three dates giggled at a table in the back corner. Lucy spotted me, waving me over. I weaved through the crowded space. This seemed to be the place to be tonight in Sweet River. As I passed the table directly across from my group, my eyes landed on...Jordan.

This town. If I wasn't running into memories of him, I was running into the literal him.

Jordan was with a few friends, not quite as giggly as my crew.

I felt torn between really hoping he'd notice me and also really hoping to remain invisible. Jordan definitely noticed me. His jaw opened in surprise before he shook his head with a smile spreading across his face. I gave a tiny shrug as I slinked into the open chair at my table.

Jordan hung his large body off his chair, leaning toward me across the slim aisle. "Great minds?" His voice sounded like an old favorite song I hadn't heard in a while but was realizing I knew beat for beat. I wanted to press repeat.

"I guess so," I said through a chuckle. I then gestured to my friends. "Some of my friends from work are having a Galentines Day."

Lucy said, "Hi." Simone smiled.

Jordan tugged his thumb toward his table. "A single support

group." The word *single* was like a knife to my chest. Jordan never felt like anything but mine.

His friends began introducing themselves. A table of men across from my table of women. And within twenty minutes, our tables were scooted together while we dug into our dinners.

His friend Ray and my friend Simone had split off from the group having their own conversation. Jordan nodded their way and raised his eyebrows, I mouthed, *Right?* And the exchange felt achingly familiar and easy.

"Okay." I twisted in my seat toward him. "How're you doing? It's been a rough few months for you."

"Cutting to the chase, huh?" Jordan asked as a server filled our glasses with more water.

"You know I like to think it's part of my charm., I said after a sip of my champagne.

"It is. Sophia, always blowing past the limits, at track meets, in conversations," Jordan said as I winced. "But, Sophie, you always do it with grace. It leaves everyone in the stands or at the table," he licked his bottom lip, "hooked."

My face flushed pink. I looked away.

"To answer your question, though, I'm okay. My buddies thought I'd need some support today, you know, after the breakup a couple months back." Jordan swirled a noodle in red sauce. "I haven't really thought about it in the past couple weeks. Honestly, the past couple months, I've been a little distracted."

"How've you been since Nana?"

"It ebbs and flows. Probably always will," he said, settling his gaze on me. "Today's been a good day, though. I'm here with friends, with you."

"Ebbs and flows," I repeated. I felt the openness in his tone, him letting me back in bit by bit. Like my keys still worked. "Not the worst Valentine's Day ever then?"

"No, no. Em's not the worst heartbreak I ever had, either," he said it casually, but it had an impact, knocking the air out of my lungs. "Now, let's hear how you're doing. It's been a big couple months for you too. You moved back. You're starting over."

I chewed a bite of cheese ravioli, thinking through my answer. "You know, it doesn't feel like starting over. It feels like coming back home after too long away. Big hugs from everyone I run into, running my old favorite paths. Reconnecting with old friends, making new ones. It's been easier than I thought."

Jordan's eyes lit at my response. "I'm so happy. I know you went through a lot before you came back."

"Yeah, when I left, I was eighteen and reeling after my dad left my mom, and it took me some time to work through everything. And I was in a relationship, a marriage, that I thought was an escape, but it left me feeling lonelier than ever. But the time after my own divorce, after the grieving, and the healing, and some therapy, that felt like *starting over.* This, this feels like..."

"A warm hug?" he asked, slipping his arm around me and pulling me in. I giggled holding my fork with a bite of ravioli on it in the air. This warmth, this ease, was something I'd missed, and after losing it, I recognized now how lucky I was to be feeling it again.

"It'd been too long away," I said as he let me go. The two of us returned to our plates. A jazzy song with saxophones crooned through the restaurant.

"Sounds like it was an important time that you needed. You can't rush things like growing. Or healing. Not everyone is going to stay in Sweet River forever. We're just lucky you came back. You left this scrappy little eighteen-year-old, and now, you're," he looked me over, "a grown woman. Still scrappy as ever." He tucked a strand of hair behind my ear. "Your hair is longer, and you've got this scar by your lip." His gaze tripped down my face, down my neck, making my heart trip. "A few new freckles across your neck."

"The scar was from a short gig as a dog walker while I was in college." I tore a piece of warm garlic bread and dragged it through softened butter. "What were you up to all this time?"

He leaned back in his chair. "I was trying to get over you," he said, and I almost choked on my bite, but he continued, "I went to school for business, which was fun. I focused hard on the work, though, not making much time for anything else. I got out of school and went straight to building up the business. I love working with my dad. I love building houses. I dated here and there. I thought Emma could be the one. It seemed like a nice story. She was sweet."

"She *seemed* sweet," I said.

"Who's sweet?" Lucy asked on the other side of me. Reminding me that Jordan and I were at a table full of people, not on an intimate date.

"Jordan's ex, Emma Brown," I said, trying to sound as un-awkward as possible.

Lucy smiled. "Oh, yeah. I know her." Unsure what to say to Jordan about his ex.

"We were talking about what we've been up to the last several years," I offered before taking a sip of water.

"Oh, I'm curious. What were you up to?" Lucy asked me. The table went quiet for me to share.

"School, for starters. I was busy getting an education degree—practicums and reading an insane number of children's books. You know about that, Lucy. I dated one guy during school. Honestly, looking back, I was trying so hard to force it. He was a musician and seemed like the perfect escape route from my own problems. We got married straight out of college." I still remembered looking in the mirror the morning of my wedding, my mom questioning, *Is this what you want?* And I thought, shouldn't I know the answer to that before I walk down the aisle?

"He was going this way with his music." I pointed one direction with my right hand. "And I was going this way." I pointed the opposite way with my left hand. "Also, I had to learn that marriage isn't something that you can use to hide away from all the hard and scary things of life—eventually, everything finds a way to seep in. And it'll tear your relationship down."

People murmured around me, but my eyes were locked on Jordan's hazel eyes.

"Like I was just telling Jordan, I had some stuff to work through. Some stuff to face. And that's exactly what I was doing the past several years. *Growing up.* Tyler and I divorced. I spent time getting to know myself again, facing all the stuff I was running from," I said.

The server reached across the table to move our empty plates.

"What brought you back? The job?" Simone asked.

"I asked myself after I finally trusted I knew the answer: what was right for me? And you know what? It was coming back here." I tapped the table in front of us. In front of Jordan.

"I'm glad you came back," Lucy said through a smile. Someone asked her if she'd ever moved away. Other people started discussing college romances.

Jordan covered my hand with his. "I'm glad you came back, too." Then he added, "And I'm proud of you for facing all the stuff you'd been running from."

"Me too." I toyed with my cloth napkin. "It's something I had to do on my own, away from all my crutches."

Jordan cleared his throat. "Sophia Rogers always wants to do it on her own."

"I *had* to do that on my own. But I realized I don't *want* to do everything alone. I missed the people here. So I came home, didn't I?"

Through a dry laugh, Jordan said, "Yes, and you have remarkable timing. You came back right when I needed some Sophie in my life."

Was that all? He just needed some Sophie a couple weeks ago? A tiny fix. While I feel like I've been needing Jordan since we were racing down our childhood streets. Since he carried me across the finish line. Since he kissed me under the mistletoe.

He was wrong thinking I had to do everything on my own. I needed to grow up and prove to myself I could do things on my own after growing up feeling like he was a fact of my life in the way my eyes were brown. Needing Jordan felt like part of my DNA.

There was some friendly group chatter. Some laughter. People got up to leave, waved goodbye, and kissed cheeks. Ray and Simone were going for coffee down the block. They didn't invite us, and we wouldn't have joined. We stayed.

Waiters came and pulled our tables apart. Jordan ordered us dessert and more drinks. We kept talking. My heart fizzed like champagne in a flute.

I was telling him about my last teaching job when I spotted Emma, Jordan's ex, and Gabriel, *together again*, at the bar. *Please leave*, I silently prayed. I was wrapped up in Jordan's attention like a cozy coat I had to myself right now, and I didn't want to share.

Gabriel and I exchanged glances. Jordan was searching for a photo on his phone to show me, and I unabashedly gave Gabriel a look of complete horror that he was here. He didn't seem thrilled to see Jordan and me either.

I saw him swallow and then turn to Emma.

Moments later, with a wine bottle in tow, they left the restaurant giggling. *Jordan was in a single support group tonight, and Emma was on a date*, I thought a little judgmentally.

But then, I looked around the table… It was only Jordan and me sharing dessert alone at a candlelit table, cheeks flushed and sharing stories. This wasn't a date, but it was *something*. And I wouldn't leave the table until he did.

"We talked about the past," Jordan said, sliding his fork through our chocolate cake. "Tell me about your future. What do you want the next decade to look like?"

I felt myself smiling. "Honestly, now that I'm nearly thirty, I'm not going to pretend about what I want anymore. I want the cozy Hallmark story. I want the loud kids in the house. A husband who makes us breakfast on the weekend. I want piles of laundry to gripe about. I want to make lessons while my husband rubs my feet, and we watch a movie. I want the family, the dog, the house." I imagined the house we used to dream of, but I didn't tell him that part. "I want the sappy, Hallmark stuff. *I just do.*"

He took in a deep breath. "I want that, too."

A candle flickered on the table and cast shadows on Jordan's elbows resting on the table. Something had crumbled between us weeks ago.

"You want piles of laundry?" I tried to make a joke.

"I'm not afraid of laundry. Or rubbing feet." *Was he talking about my laundry, my feet?* I almost asked, but there was still a delicate history between us. Something to handle with care.

We didn't leave until the waiters began sweeping the floors and locking the doors. Until they told us they were closing soon.

I bundled my coat in the darkened restaurant.

"Wow, I didn't realize this would be such a late night." Jordan patted his pockets making sure he had his wallet and keys.

"Me neither." I followed him to the door.

The server unlocked it for us, urging us to "Stay dry."

We stepped out into the pouring rain. The sidewalks cleared of people with everyone taking cover. Storm and streetlights and us.

Jordan squinted through the water. "I'm glad we ran into each other," he said, his voice raised over the downpour. "Glad we got to spend another Valentine's Day together."

"Me too," I nearly shouted. I raised an arm over my face so I could look up at him. His hazel eyes looked amber, and his sandy hair soaked. He was so much better than my memories.

"It's nice to know you're doing well back home. Back here." He took a step closer to me. "You know, we could hang out sometimes?"

"Not just keep running into each other?" I said trying to smile, my teeth starting to chatter from the cold seeping through my wet clothes.

"If you ever want to..." There was yearning in his voice, a

question, but also hesitance. I wanted to push through it like a door.

"I *do* want to," I said quickly. Maybe too quickly. I didn't care.

He nodded. "Yeah?"

"Yeah," I said, almost forcefully. I stepped closer. He ran his hand over his face to clear away the water.

The two of us were stuck in place, freezing and drenched, like we had cement in our shoes instead of rain. Like it was useless to try and keep us apart.

A few silent beats passed. A car drove down the street splashing water in its wake. A couple ran down the sidewalk squealing in the rain to their car.

"We probably look crazy out here," Jordan said, his eyes still on me. "Why..."

"I guess we missed each other," I offered. A feeble, tiny, minimization of the feelings between us.

It hurt when we separated. Every single time. Even tonight.

"I guess so," he murmured, thoughtful. "I don't want Sweet River Elementary needing to call in a sub because their favorite new teacher is sick."

I laughed softly. "A little rain doesn't hurt," I said through chattering teeth. He raised a hand toward me, and I knew that little shoulder rub he was about to do so well I started to lean into it...but before making contact he dropped his hand.

He took a step back. "I'm this way." He pointed behind himself in the opposite direction of where I was parked.

"I'm that way." I nodded behind me.

"See you around, Sophie?"

"Not if I see you first," I said as he turned on his feet and sloshed his way toward his truck.

I stood there another minute, not ready to leave the perfect little Valentine bubble we'd shared. A car door slammed shut. I shook my head, waking myself from the haze, and stumbled through the puddled streets to my car.

Chapter 11

DECEMBER 23RD, 2023

My doorbell rings, I'm wrapped up in a special satin robe gifted to me for today. I skip from my spot in the bathroom stationed in front of my skincare products lined up.

"A special delivery?" Mom asks with a twinkle in her eyes, joining me on my trip toward the door. We race toward it squealing together.

I feel giddy, light, as I open the door to the cold winter air. No one is standing there, but instead, a tiny silver box with a red bow is waiting on the doorstep. I pick it up. I can smell the snow on the ground mingling with my fresh pine Christmas wreath as I start to eagerly undo the bow.

"Come inside to the warmth," Mom giggles as she pulls me into the house, closing the door behind me.

I remove the bow, then lift the lid to find a shiny gold locket inside. I scoop the locket up, dangling it from my fingers. I knew this locket. The feel of it was familiar to me. It used to hold a picture of Herb inside when it hung from Nana Silk's neck. I open the two sides of the locket, to find it now holds a picture of Jordan and me, dressed up for our pretend wedding as little kids.

Tears drop from my eyes, one by one. I hold the locket close to my chest, knowing everything this gift meant, not only for the two of us, but for his family. In that moment, with all our twists and turns, I wouldn't change a word of our story.

MARCH 4TH, 2023

JORDAN

I hope the new favorite teacher didn't catch a
cold last night after our dinner

ME

No worries. Miss Sophia showed up to work
this morning bright and early and healthy

ok, maybe not bright…or early. But definitely
healthy!

JORDAN

Good to hear. Had to check on ya, Sophie

thanks for being better than any valentine
support group 😌

One March morning, I woke up to the sound of children's
squeals and shouts, parents clapping, and the distinct
thud of a soccer ball being kicked. *Ah,* I realized. Saturday soccer
for the pre-K kiddos had begun across the street.

I hopped from my bed to my bedroom window to confirm,

peeking through my mini blinds. Children were racing around in baggy tee shirts with glee, parents passing out juice boxes, and there was the finest soccer coach I'd ever seen standing in the midst of it all. I opened the blinds wider, taking in how well Jordan could pull off a baseball cap and sweatshirt when he looked straight toward me and cocked his head to the side curiously.

He couldn't see me... Could he? I stepped back quickly, the blinds snapping shut.

I tiptoed out of my room to the kitchen even though no one could hear me. I tightened my robe as my coffee maker whirred to life.

My morning was quiet and calm as I ate my breakfast and tried to pretend Jordan wasn't steps outside my window, even as my heart rocketed around inside my chest. I decided the best course of action was to proceed normally and don my usual running attire for my Saturday morning run. I did my pre-run stretch in my living room.

I walked out the front door and saw practice wrapping up in the park. Parents were picking up tired three-year-olds and packing up snack bags. I waited on my front porch, pretending to prepare a playlist or something on my phone, trying to muster up the courage to go over and say hi to Jordan after the mini blind moment.

Or maybe I could just pretend to casually run by him?

I glanced his way sneakily. He was crouching down talking to a group of kids. The group grinned to themselves and snickered.

I tucked my phone into my armband and started stretching my legs behind me. A little extra warm-up never hurt anyone.

"MISS SOPHIA! MISS SOPHIA!" I stopped what I was doing and jerked my head toward the park where little voices were shouting my name in unison.

"COACH JORDAN WANTS TO..." more excited whisper-ing, then, "DRINK COFFEE WITH YOU!" This shouting was followed by tons of laughter. The kids beamed with pride as Jordan high-fived each one.

My cheeks literally hurt from smiling so wide at the utter cuteness. I immediately raced down my front porch steps. Running across the street to the sound of cheers from the kids and parents.

"COACH JORDAN, SHE'S COMING OVER HERE!" a little boy shouted.

"Will you? Will you drink coffee with him?" A tiny girl with pigtails asked when she saw me, cutting in between Jordan and me.

Jordan's gaze was on me. He bit his lower lip. "I would love to have coffee with Coach Jordan," I said, looking straight at him. Spotting the soccer ball a few feet from us, I added, "On one condition."

"What's that?" Jordan asked, crossing his arms.

"I think you should show off some of your moves for the kids." I placed my hands on my hips.

"How do you reckon?"

"Well..." I started to take a few slow steps toward the ball, and he lifted a brow. I shuffled the ball while I said, "Come and get it?"

The remaining kids squealed, and their parents laughed. One mom said, "Jordan, you've met your match!"

He was breathless, chasing after me, as he said in reply, "Oh, this one has always kept me on my toes—sometimes, *literally!*"

I was kicking the ball as he chased me down the field, heart racing from the run, racing from his throaty laughter. He caught the ball from me and started down the field. I decided I didn't want to play fair and leaped on his back.

Our audience was laughing, as he yelled, "Rule violation!"

But he had his hands gripped around the backs of my thighs, my skin warm where we touched, my arms laced around his neck. The two of us laughed ourselves breathless.

"What are you teaching the kids, Miss Sophia?" he asked gravelly.

"Distraction," I whispered as I swung my body around his landing between him and the ball. I kicked it across the field. The kids cheered while I lifted my arms in victory. Jordan lifted me up and threw me over his shoulder so easily like he was tossing on a scarf as he ran after the ball, catching it as it rolled across the field. His shoulder muscles moved underneath me. He dribbled the ball, then hopped it between both feet before giving it a big kick in the other direction—all with me over his shoulder. He slid me down his body. We were both sweaty and panting, chest to chest.

The few remaining from the team clapped, and parents bid their goodbyes to us and each other while we were still catching our breaths. And I was trying to stuff down the desire to climb back on him.

"You're still a showoff," I said.

"You said the deal was to *show off* my moves," he said, spreading his arms out. "Did I earn my coffee date?"

Date. My heart caught. "You put in the effort."

I helped him clean while he told me about his first practice. He was bright and excited with a smile on his face that he couldn't contain—a smile I'd missed desperately. I loved the way he loved coaching these kids.

Finally, as he slammed his truck door after the final load, he looked at me and said, "Where to for that cup of coffee?"

"I know a spot," I said, grabbing his hand and leading him across the street to my house.

M y kitchen suddenly felt tiny once Jordan with his miles of broad shoulders and long legs was standing inside it. I tried to calm my excited little heart bouncing around and busy myself with making coffee.

I could feel his warmth when he walked up behind me, his

breath inches away from my neck. I lost count as I spooned ground coffee into the filter.

"What kind of coffee you got there?" he asked.

My hands were so jittery coffee spilled from the spoon. We both ignored it.

"What are you a fancy coffee snob now?" I scooted to the side so he could see for himself. "Is that good enough for you?"

"I've used an espresso machine for the last couple years."

"No." I gasped, returning to the coffee machine. "Do you use the tiny cups, too?" I snorted at the picture of a tiny espresso cup in Jordan's big hands. I poured water into the dispenser.

"Sometimes," he said, taking a step closer to me. "And it's good, Sophie."

"Mhmm," I hummed. *Click.* I turned on the coffee machine.

"Maybe I should make you a cup some morning?" he said. A bright idea. I was pretty sure if Jordan was making it, I would like it. "I can still add cinnamon."

I twirled around. My back was against the kitchen counter. Jordan put an arm around each side of me and hunched his shoulders so we were face to face.

"Now you're a fancy espresso drinker." I raised my chin. "What else is new?"

He took a step back, crossing his arms. "Well, I like plants." I felt cold in his body's absence.

"You like plants now? You're a plant daddy?"

He grabbed my hands as if pleading with me. "I don't know what that is, but please don't call me that ever again."

"Okay, so what do you mean you *like plants*?" I cocked my head, my ponytail falling across my shoulder.

"I have maybe ten different potted plants around my place. They each have their own schedule with the sun and water. I've done this for years now. I like the routine of it."

"Did you name them?" I felt a pang in my chest, dying to know the plant routine.

He just grinned. I knew Jordan. He'd definitely named them. "Now, you. Tell me something new."

"Something new." I tapped my chin thoughtfully. *He* felt like something new and something familiar all at once. "I've gotten super into reading mysteries and thrillers. I can't get enough. I'll read one a night sometimes."

Jordan laughed. "You say this like you're admitting an addiction—"

I grabbed his hand and led him back through the living room, then turned into my bedroom. I pointed at the bookshelves lining the wall stuffed with books. His eyes went wide at the sheer volume.

"I never knew you were this into mysteries." He walked in and perused the spines. "What a collection."

"I never knew I was into them either. But my first year of teaching felt so stressful and exhausting, I needed an outlet. An escape. Another teacher raved about this Gillian Flynn book and lent it to me... I haven't stopped since. They're my treat."

Jordan was beaming down at me as if every word I said was sunshine he wanted to soak in. "Tell me what else is new with you."

"Um," I hummed. "Well, I changed running shoe brands. I'm officially a Brooks girl." I shrugged.

"You're copying me now?" he said. We used to argue over which running shoe was superior. After I moved, when it came time to buy a new pair, I found myself buying his brand. A silly way to stay closer to him. Every morning when I went for a run, I'd see my sneakers, and it was like he was still joining me in some tiny way.

"You were right about 'em. I can't go back."

He bit his lip. "I've got one for you, Sophie." His eyes twinkled with mischief. "I'm a Swiftie."

I peered at him critically. I adored Taylor Swift—always had. He used to tease me and turn down the volume when I played her. It was a point of playful contention during our entire relationship.

"I don't believe you. You're kidding."

"'Speak Now' is probably my favorite. I mean, 'Folklore' is amazing, but 'Speak Now,' just hits here," he patted his chest earnestly. "'Mine?' 'Last Kiss?' 'Long Live?'"

"Since when?" I gasped.

He shrugged in reply, the corners of his mouth tugging into a grin. His eyes tripped down my outfit. "You're in your Brooks now."

"Well, I was going to go for a run, then this whole team of little soccer players started shouting my name." I leaned against my doorway.

"I didn't mean to interrupt your run," Jordan said.

"It's no problem." The nutty smell of coffee crept into the room. "I think our coffee is ready, anyway."

He followed me back to the kitchen.

"You still take two spoons of sugar, no milk?"

"Yeah, yeah," he said. "Some things never change." And this, for whatever reason, tugged on my heart so strong tears pricked my eyes.

So much time had passed since we'd been in each other's lives. We'd forged new lives with new habits and new memories. Other relationships had been built and broken since *us*. Yet, some things hadn't changed—like his inky, sweet coffee. Or how his smile broke out over his face as if he never could contain it. Whatever string had tied me to him still hung between us. It tugged me to him, hung me on his every word, this string unbroken, after all this time.

He reached over me toward the cupboards and pulled down two mugs with my back against his chest for a moment. I poured his mug full and dropped two sugars in. Jordan's scent still lingered near me even though he'd walked across the kitchen by now.

I turned to find him in my fridge with my carton of half and half. He raised a brow in question.

I nodded. "Like you said, some things never change."

By the time our mugs were empty, Jordan and I were sitting on my front porch, the two of us side by side on the front steps. He kicked my Brooks with his own pair. "I have to admit I'm dying to see you put these bad boys to use."

"You sure?" I had my arms around my knees, peeking a glance up at him. "You can't cheat in a race. Can't throw me over your shoulder to win."

Jordan chuckled. "Sure, Sophie, that's why I picked you up earlier. To win."

My cheeks flushed.

"You want to meet up next Saturday after practice and go for a run? I'll bring my running shoes." A twinkle in his eye.

"Sure, we'll see who's faster now." I bumped my shoulder against his.

He bumped me right back. And everything in me felt warm and right, even if just for a moment.

MARCH 11TH, 2023

JORDAN
SENT PICTURE OF A COZY MYSTERY BOOK

look what I found

ME

OH MY that's one I've been wanting

JORDAN

got it, I'll bring it Sat

ME

Jordan, you don't have to do that!

JORDAN

gotta make sure you got treats stocked for those stressful days

ME

well, it was a stressful day, I'll admit

JORDAN

See? Good thing I got it then. So, what happened?

Next Saturday, I anxiously padded around my house until I could hear car doors slamming shut outside and people shouting their goodbyes to Coach Jordan.

I slipped outside my front door and hopped across the street. When Jordan's eyes landed on mine, a grin broke across his face.

I grinned, too. After all this time, all these years, and all the different Sophies I've been, I could still make him smile as big as the Texas sky.

"I've got my Brooks in my truck." He jerked a thumb toward where he parked.

I stood in front of him and wiggled a foot in front of him, showing off my shoes.

His eyes slowly worked their way up from my feet, and he said, "No way I'm looking as good as you in 'em, but I'll go get 'em."

The two of us kept pace, as easy as slipping on your old favorite jeans. Our shoes slapped against the pavement and the crisp spring breeze blew across our shoulders as our breath caught a rhythm.

I didn't have to tell him the path. He knew these streets by the school as well as his route back home.

Our eyes kept finding one another, my shoulder bumping into his arm. High from running, high from each other. The conversation between us was as natural and rhythmic as our stride.

"I'd missed this," I said, nearing the end of our lap. I'd been running alone all these years.

"Me too," he said, looking out at the path ahead of us.

I felt reckless and giddy being around him, better than endorphins like I could run at full speed and win a race, so I ran ahead.

He shouted after me, "Where are you going?"

I turned around so I was running backward, facing him.

"Show off," he said but in a way that made it sound like a compliment, making my stomach dip.

He ran up toward me, jogging at my side. "Think you can keep up?" I teased, spinning around to run full speed ahead.

"Oh, I'll find a way every time." He laughed, breathless as he ran after me. "You know that about me."

And maybe he was right—maybe he could always find a way to catch up with me, no matter the speed, no matter the years between us.

Quickly, he was at my side, meeting my stride. His eyes danced over to mine.

I was out of breath, my pace slowing. We'd come back around to the park. I ran up onto the grass, pulling him down with me as I fell against the grass.

We didn't land gracefully, the two of us on our backs facing the sky. Elm trees waved overhead. Panting, I twisted onto my side to face Jordan. He was out of breath, too, with sweat on his brow.

His gaze focused on me, a quiet question behind his eyes.

"What are you thinking?" I asked, brushing a loose strand of hair behind my ear.

"You shouldn't be allowed to look that good running. It's distracting for a man just trying to keep up. Unfair advantage," he said breathless.

I cracked up, burying myself against his chest on old instinct. He pulled me in close, though, giving me a squeeze. He smelled like his familiar piney, sweaty self.

"You don't like an easy race, anyway, Jordan. You never have." I noticed something dark looping down from his shoulder. "What's this?" I brushed it with my fingertips.

"Oh," he said, then pulled up his sleeve to reveal a tattoo. "Another something new."

"You've got a tattoo?" I said, taking in the compass pointing toward Sweet River's coordinates.

"A few," he said, then lifted his shirt to reveal his chest with a family tree on his right chest about the size of his fist, his family's names along the roots. And then right above it, under his right shoulder in thick, dark letters was the name of his childhood street, *our* childhood street—Avalon Lane. Without thinking, I traced it with my fingertips, making him shudder.

"Our street?" Tears pricked my eyes. Something I'd avoided for so long, suddenly so sweet when I viewed it in this new way.

"I wanted to honor everything that made me who I am today," he said, his voice low and warm. "My street. And the girl down the street. I'll always carry it here." He pressed my hand against the spot where the tattoo was on his chest. His skin was warm. His chest was solid against my hand.

"I wear that scar on my knee from when I fell during the race like that, too. It's never faded away, and I never want it to," I said quietly, pulling my hand from his chest and mindlessly reaching for my knee. "I still love every single one of our memories."

"Me, too," he said, pulling his shirt back down. "We were each other's whole world."

I nodded. Unable to say how much that meant to me. Hoping he could feel it in how I wrapped my arms tight around him.

He squeezed my side, making me laugh and squirm, until we were tangled up there on the grass sweaty, breathless, him leaning over me. My eyes were on his lips. I knew how they tasted—how they felt. *Or was that something else new?*

I looked into his eyes, and they were taking me in. His brows were creased as if in near agony. Like he was torn. Like he knew better than to be playing with fire this way. Like he'd been here before, and it all burned up last time.

But then he pinned me onto my back on the grass and kissed me anyway. Needy, as if in the press of his body against mine, the pull of his lips, the grip of his hands on me, he'd channel every ounce of missing me.

It was the gasping, frantic kind of kissing. The "I've missed you so badly I could kiss you forever" kind of kissing.

He ran his hands in my hair, moving his mouth from my lips to my cheek, then down my neck, until he found his way back to my mouth. I ran my hands through his hair and down his back, pulling him closer.

He rasped, "*Sophie.*"

With his forehead pressed over mine, our noses brushing, my skin afire, I gasped, "I've missed you so badly."

He opened his eyes, and we looked at each other. This wasn't just playing with fire anymore. This was consuming. We both knew it.

He swallowed. Then sat up, running his hand over his face. I stayed there on the grass, looking at the sky, resisting the urge to pull him back down to me.

"We've got to figure some stuff out, huh?" he said gruffly. "I need to pump the brakes for a second."

I was the one who always pushed harder when the finish line was in sight, but I forced myself to take a breath and slow down for him, for us.

Chapter 14

SATURDAYS IN SPRING 2023

For the next few weeks, I spent every Saturday morning watching Jordan coach pre-K soccer then we went for a run. These last few times without a make-out session in the middle of the park. Afterward, we'd get lunch together.

One time, he helped me grocery shop, and we bickered over my shopping list like an old married couple. On the third Saturday in April, Jordan sat in my living room after we made sandwiches and played his favorite Taylor Swift songs.

I shook my head at him. "I can't believe you finally got into her after all the times I tried!"

"Come on." He was lying across my couch, ankles crossed, head on a pillow. His eyes were closed as "Mine" blasted from my speakers.

Every inch of my body itched to curl up beside him.

"You didn't leave me much to hold onto from you. She was one of those few things."

My mouth went dry. I was curled up in an armchair parallel to the couch. I thought of my feet in his favorite kind of shoes. How I'd made his favorite pasta sometimes when I missed him. Or slip on the navy sweatshirt of his I never did mail back. "I get it."

"I'd play it in the car, and sometimes, it was like you were sitting across from me again singing along with the melody." He played with the hem of his shirt.

I was giving us the time to figure out whatever it was we were figuring out. Like pacing ourselves during a marathon so we didn't burn out too quickly again. But as we sat across from each other with the afternoon light glimmering through my living room blinds, I wondered—*what else was there left to figure out?*

I still want him running beside me.

He still wants me in the passenger seat of his truck.

That evening, he was walking down my porch steps, and I hated him leaving, so I grabbed his hand, yanking him to a stop.

"Sophie?" he asked.

I wrapped my arms around his waist, burying my face in his chest. He slid his arms around me tight like he didn't want to let go. A breeze rustled my hair against my back. A couple of kids squealed in the park across the street, but it felt like it was just the two of us.

"Sophie," he whispered against the top of my ear, sending goosebumps across my skin.

"I missed you then. I miss you *now*," I said, muffled by his tee shirt.

"I thought I was going to miss you forever," he said back. He scooped his hands around the back of my head and brought his face closer to mine as I lifted up onto my toes.

He kissed my chin softly. "I missed this chin," he whispered. He kissed both cheeks. "The freckles on these cheeks." He kissed my nose. "The way your nose scrunches when you think you've got me beat." Then he brushed his lips against my forehead before whispering, "Everything. I missed every single thing about you."

My mom's car pulled up in front of my house, behind Jordan's truck, waking us from our heady haze. I licked my lips, saying, "My mom's here for Sunday supper."

Mom and I had started a tradition of having Sunday dinners together—taking turns at our houses. Tonight was my night to host, but she would bring over the ingredients and teach me a new recipe from her and Nonna's shared recipe collection. "You could join us?"

Jordan shook his head, hands still in my hair. "I'm leaving for a work trip tomorrow morning really early. I need to go pack. I won't be back until Friday night. But I'll be there Saturday morning for the last soccer meet for the spring." He focused his eyes on mine. "Meet me after?"

Thursday night I got a fever after a bad cold had spread across my classroom. Friday morning, I stayed home from work, barely even leaving the bed for food, praying I would wake up on Saturday refreshed and ready to tell Jordan how I felt for him.

Saturday morning, the sun blazed in through my curtains making me squint in pain, my head throbbing. I kicked off the sheets, sweaty and feverish. Coughing fits and a runny nose kept waking me up throughout the night, but I felt too weak to get out of bed to find medicine.

I heard little kids shouting goodbye outside my window. I leaped out of bed, body aching, knowing I'd slept way later than I'd wanted. Today was a big deal to Jordan. We'd been text messaging the day before as he tried to decide if the kids would prefer he made them sprinkle cookies or chocolate chip to celebrate the last day.

He'd texted me before I fell asleep double-checking if I'd be there, but I didn't want to say I was sick. I was determined to wake up feeling better. To wrap him up in my arms after the final soccer day and tell him I want every Saturday from now on.

I scrambled to the mirror. My nose was as red as Rudolph's. My room was full of scattered used tissues. I tried to tame my hair the best I could and yanked on leggings and a sweater.

Dazed and sniffly, I ran out to find Jordan alone in the park packing his truck.

"Hey, sleepyhead," he greeted me as I walked across the park to his truck. "The kids loved the cookies. But they missed Miss Sophia."

"I'm sorry. I overslept." I sniffled. I leaned down to grab a case of water bottles to help put away.

His forehead wrinkled as he looked at me. "Sophie? Are you okay?"

"I have a cold, I think," I admitted, leaving the water bottles on the ground as he placed a hand on my forehead. "I'm so sad I missed your last day. I'm sorry."

"Oh, you're burning hot," he gasped. "We need to get you inside." Jordan left his truck and everything behind, scooping me into his arms and carrying me back to my house.

My mind was blurry, my body achy as Jordan tucked me into my bed.

"You were still going to try and help me pack up the truck, weren't you, Rogers?" Jordan said softly.

Rogers. My sick, tired heart soared. He pulled the quilt up under my chin as I shivered.

I closed my eyes for a moment, opening them back up to find him swiping a thermometer across my forehead. "Too high," he said gruffly.

Next thing I knew, I had a cold rag on my head.

I closed my eyes again, opening them to find Jordan setting a warm mug of tea beside me. "Drink this. I added honey for your throat," he said.

From my room, I could hear him in the kitchen rustling around in my medicine cabinet.

He made me scrambled eggs on buttered toast. I had vivid memories of a younger Jordan sick under a fuzzy blanket on his family's couch while his mom delivered him plates of freshly cooked scrambled eggs on toast.

It was as if I had been a wilted flower and Jordan was the sun peeking out from behind the clouds beaming down on me, bringing me back to life. I was already feeling so much better.

I took a bite of toast as Jordan set a fresh glass of water down on my end table. "You know, you obviously remind me of your dad. With the sandy hair. And the love for building things. And the way you two are both always the most welcoming presence in whatever room you enter."

He stood by the bed, head cocked to the side.

"But, days like today when you make me food and tuck me into bed, you remind me of your mom. She was always the first to clean up my scraped knees or comfort me on a bad day. You're like that, too. You attune to everyone's needs, whether it's physical like getting them cough syrup, or it's emotional, like how you kept checking in on me since I've moved back."

"The checking in is a little selfish." Jordan sat down on the end of the bed. "I can't resist any reason to talk to you."

"It's not just that, though. You've always been there for me. You didn't want me to go to school hours away, but you still worked on the college application with me for hours. You even threw me a big party to celebrate when I got in. If things hadn't..." I let my voice trail off. I had a lump in my throat but kept speaking. "I know you would've driven miles and miles every weekend to see me."

Jordan embodied the healthy kind of love where in his atmosphere my needs always rose to the surface. He never let me bury them. A younger me didn't realize how rare it was to be loved like that. Older me? I was ready to dig his needs and wants up like buried treasure.

He looked down at the quilt on my bed. "You know I love this town—I love my business—but I would've left it all and moved to you. I was already thinking about it even then. Nothing would've kept me from you."

Nothing would've kept him from me, *except me* it turned out.

"Can I say I'm happy you didn't leave everything?" I whispered, not sure if what I was saying would be received how I meant it. "I love how you give. How you care. But you deserve to have a life about you, too. I see how working with your dad makes you happy. How driving down the streets of Sweet River is exactly where you should be. I wouldn't have wanted to be the person who took that away from you."

Maybe our younger selves weren't meant for each other yet because we weren't equipped for the depth of our feelings back then. Instead, older Jordan, who'd finally realized he wanted someone whose dreams matched his, was meant for older Sophia who'd come back to Sweet River on her own accord because she grew up and realized all her dreams were here.

"Sophie, you wouldn't have taken anything from me. It's funny. You're saying how I've always been there for you and would've driven miles to see you...as if that wasn't also *for me*. Because there's nothing, not my hometown, not my job, nothing that makes me happier than seeing you smile." Jordan's gaze was so intent I could nearly feel it on my skin. "But, maybe, I was young then and didn't quite know how to navigate what we had between us."

Maybe we could navigate it now, I wanted to say, trying to collect my fuzzy, NyQuil-laden thoughts enough to broach the subject.

But Jordan was standing up. "Get some sleep," he said gently, taking my empty plate. "We can talk later."

After he returned the dish to the sink, he came back to find me sitting up on the bed.

"Will you sit down beside me?" I asked with a sniffly voice.

"Of course, Rogers." He plopped down beside me, and I nestled into his side. After all these years, I still fit in the nook of his neck just right.

"Wanna watch a movie?" he asked, reaching for the remote.

I nodded.

"Which one?" he asked.

I only murmured into his chest, too tired to think. My symptoms were declining, but now my body was demanding sleep.

Next thing I knew, Julia Roberts and Richard Gere were on the tiny TV screen on the dresser across from my bed. You couldn't go wrong with Julia and Richard. Jordan ran his fingers through my hair until I was lulled asleep.

L ater, the sun was setting outside my window. The movie was over. Jordan had one of my thrillers in his lap and his arm looped around me. I felt so wholly content.

It felt so good, so right to wake up beside Jordan Silk. To have his ankles crossed, all comfort and warmth, relaxing on my bed. My eyes began to pool with tears—to have something, even if for only a moment, that I'd thought I'd lost forever.

He noticed my waking movements and glanced over at me. "Hey there. Good nap?"

"The best," I whispered. Still shivering.

"That's good. I have the thermometer right here." He snatched it off the end table on his side of the bed. "Let's check your temp."

He rested one hand lightly under my jaw as he used the other to swipe my forehead. His fingertips rough against my skin. Maybe it was my fever, but every touch felt magnified. "Seems your fever has dropped a lot. That's good, but let's still get you some medicine."

After I took more medicine, I shuffled into the kitchen to find him warming a jar of Nonna's Minestrone soup on the stove.

My thinking was still kind of fuzzy, and the rules were still kind of fuzzy, so I thought, *Forget the rules*. I walked over to him, wrapping my arms around his waist and resting my head on his chest under the kitchen light.

"My sick Sophie." He ran his rough fingers through my hair, resting his hands against my shoulders. "You should be in bed."

"I should be with you," I whispered, my voice a scrape.

He wrapped me in close. "I'm right here."

"Don't leave, okay?" I said, my filter gone.

. . .

The clock on my nightstand blinked *two a.m.* when I woke up. My head finally felt clearer. My skin was no longer sweaty and no shivers. My nose and throat had felt better hours ago. I felt revived.

Jordan was asleep over the covers, laying on his back, still in his soccer coach get-up of running shorts and a sweatshirt.

I was deciding if I should wake him up to send him home or let the man sleep after being my caretaker for hours when he turned and opened his eyes to me watching him. He gave a sleepy smile, another favorite of mine.

"You stayed," I said, breaking the quietness of night.

"I did," he said, his voice raw with emotion and sleep.

I sat up beside him, placing a hand against his cheek. "Jordan." He closed his eyes, turning his face into my hand. "The past few years felt like holding my breath and being near you feels like I can *finally* exhale."

He kissed the inside of my palm, as I said, "Thank you for taking care of me today."

"You don't have to thank me. I want to be here." He wrapped his hand around my wrist and pulled me closer to him. He ran his thumb over my forehead. "You still feel cooler."

"I think my fever dropped for good." I sat on my folded knees, my body square against his.

He ran his hands down my arms, leaving a trail of goosebumps in their wake.

"You're a good doctor."

"You're a good patient," he said gruffly. "Actually, not really. You were torturing me all day."

"Torturing you?"

"I'm trying to respect this relationship we have here, trying to take my time to figure *us* out, but it's torture trying to keep my hands to myself." He gestured to where I sat beside him, my long hair a mess down my shoulders. "Like, look at you. I feel like a man who'd finally kicked his caffeine addiction, and someone is roasting their favorite beans. And they know exactly..." he let his voice fade.

"How it tastes?"

His eyes were agonized as he asked, his voice so low it echoed through me, "Do you want me to keep my hands to myself?"

I shook my head no.

He grabbed my hands and pulled me onto his lap, and then I pulled away. "Wait, wait," I hated the words as they left my mouth. "Jordan, I've been sick. I just broke my fever—"

"Please, make me sick. Give me whatever you got. I'll take it happily." He brought my lips to his and said between kisses, "Because I've missed these lips." He ran his fingers down my sides and said his words hot and breathless against my lips, "I've missed every inch of you. Every single day. For years."

I'd kissed this man thousands of times. His lips were almost as familiar to me as my own, yet tonight each kiss felt so monumental. My own personal earthquake, everything in me falling to pieces. No one else could kiss me like this—touch me like this.

It was like he hadn't forgotten anything about me. He remembered how to make me shiver. He'd remembered to kiss along my jaw, grinning when I sighed. Holding onto me like he'd been waiting for this moment for years, his hands needy against my skin.

"I wish I could have all of your Saturdays," I said between kisses.

He mumbled into my neck, "Rogers, you've always gotten whatever you wanted from me, giving you my Saturdays is like asking for pennies."

When we were teenagers, kissing till we fogged up the truck windows, he'd whisper, "Rogers, I just love you so much."

And sometimes I'd find it hard to speak. I didn't know the words to communicate just how downright into my core happy I was he was in my life. How lucky I felt he lived down my street and went to my school and loved me right back.

I was speechless now, too. Finding it hard to communicate,

except through my hands in his hair, kissing his lips till they bruised.

I was feverish again—this time just for him, incurably not even trying to resist it.

"Okay then, I'll take every single day if they're up for grabs." I pulled away for a minute, taking in this messy-haired, swollen lips view of him grinning back at me.

He ran his thumb over my bottom lip and I asked, my voice shaking as I pushed myself to expose all the feelings I've carried with me for years like battle scars, "Are they, up for grabs?"

He stilled for a moment, thumb still on my lip as I continued speaking, "I've been wanting to ask you... Have you figured it out?"

"Us?"

"Yeah, us." I nodded, hovering over him, my hair grazing against his chest. "Figured us out."

A phone rang into the night. We both startled. Both of us turned to where it was on the nightstand—it was Jordan's phone. "It should be on night mode if it's ringing..." He shook his head. I crawled off him as he rolled to the other end of the bed.

"Dad?" he answered, breathless. The clock blinked 3:04 a.m. I'd felt like I was in a timeless vortex. "What?" he gasped, standing up.

"No, I can get there." He shuffled around the room, hair a mess, jaw tight.

He hung up his phone and took a long breath, eyes closed.

"Jordan?" I asked, my mouth dry when he opened his eyes.

"I've got to go." He started walking toward the doorway. "One of our builds caught fire. Dad is there with some of the team right now, it's a..." He stopped in his tracks and looked at me. I didn't want him to go. I'm sure it was all over my face. "I know we were just..."

I wanted to say something, anything, while I still had him here, even just yell, *I'm still in love with you!* but as I opened my mouth—

His phone rang again, he looked down at it. "I've got to take this." He put his phone to his ear, answering as he ran out of the room.

Seconds later, my front door closed with a thud.

Jordan was racing toward a house on fire. Part of me wanted to throw on my shoes and follow him to make sure he stayed safe. Instead, I paced my house hoping he'd come straight back to me once it was all said and done.

He'd said I'd always gotten whatever I wanted from him. Well, what if what I wanted was *him*?

Chapter 15

APRIL 23RD, 2023

There was no way I could go to sleep that night, tossing and turning in the wee hours of the morning. No longer sick with a cold. Instead, I was sick over Jordan. Sick with worry about him at a house fire, sick at the abrupt end of our conversation.

I buried my head in my pillow. If I scoured the past few weeks for clues, he had to feel the same. He'd kissed me senseless. He'd stood in the rain with me, and I knew in my bones he didn't want to leave my side that night either. He'd spent every Saturday with me. And I was the one he needed when he was at his lowest—*my* hand he held onto for dear life.

I tried to call him as the hours passed, but it kept going straight to voicemail. Either his phone had died, or he was still busy with the fire and had to ignore my calls. I waited until the sun was finally rising outside my window to try giving his mom a call, but she didn't answer either.

I didn't even know what project they were at or how to find it, but I kicked off my blankets and got out of bed. I couldn't stay in my house.

. . .

There was no answer at his apartment door. His truck wasn't in the parking lot.

I drove the gravel dirt road that led me to Jordan's family home, but there were no cars parked out front.

My car crept through Downtown Sweet River this sleepy Sunday morning, the wind blowing my dark tresses in the wind. *Was I pushing too hard?* Sophie pounding her feet against the pavement, stretching farther with her end goal in line of sight? Reaching for Jordan whether he was ready for it or not?

Katie Hernandez was outside Coffees & Commas, flipping the sign over the door from Closed to Open when she spotted me and waved. The downtown streets were empty as I pointed my car toward home.

I parked my car in my driveway and hit the call button again —still no answer. *Should I call his sisters for an update on the fire?* They'd seemed so distant since I came back. My phone felt heavy in my hand. The sky was pink and tangerine in the morning light.

My phone vibrated in my hand. I swiped to answer before even reading who the caller was.

"Hello?"

"Sophie?" Orlando greeted me.

"Oh, hey." My voice dropped.

"I know it's early, but I'm actually getting ready to go with this girl I like to her church this morning, and I wanted your opinion on shirts. Button down or polo?" My phone beeped. I glanced at the screen where he'd sent a photo of each shirt.

I sniffled. "Button down. You always look nice in navy."

It was quiet for a beat. "Soph, I've never heard anyone say a compliment like they were saying they'd just been dumped. Are you okay?"

"It's early,"

"You're still in bed?" He sounded far away like he'd set the phone down to change.

"No." I glanced out my window. "I'm in my car."

"Soph," he chastised me through an echo.

"I'm worried for Jordan. He was over last night and had to run out the door really late because one of his builds caught fire—and I haven't heard from him since."

"I'm sure he's okay. He wasn't going to run into the fire or anything. He was probably talking and answering questions with the fireman and police and stuff, yeah?"

I nodded against the phone. "I know. My calls keep going to voicemail."

"How many times have you called?"

"Several." I sighed.

A beat passed. "How late was he at your house?"

"Like...three a.m."

"What?" He sounded closer like he'd pulled the phone back to his ear. "You guys talking again?"

"We were right in the middle of talking actually—"

"Typical three a.m. chats with pals?" he said sarcastically.

"I was sick, and he came over to take care of me—"

"Taking care of you when you're sick, *noted.*"

"And we'd both passed out. Then we woke up and realized it was late, and we started talking about our feelings. And that's when he got a call and had to run out."

"So you're worried about the fire but also worried about the talk." Orlando's tone switched from quizzical to concerned. "Worried or *Sophie obsessing*?"

"Obsessing. Of course." I clicked off my seatbelt.

"Can you give me a rundown of what you were discussing *in the middle of the night* while ill?"

"I woke up and was feeling better. I told him how being near him felt like...coming up for air. We kissed—"

"Coming up for air? That's like poetic stuff there, Soph," he said before the whirring of his electric toothbrush sounded on the other line.

"We'd actually kissed a few weeks ago but decided we needed to cool it so we could figure things out. So after we kissed again last night, where he repeatedly told me he'd missed me, I asked if he felt he'd figured anything out—"

"He obviously had figured out he'd missed you," he said through a mouthful of toothpaste.

"Right? But I don't know." I rubbed my forehead. "I'm nervous he was caught up in the moment and when we talk again, he'll have come back to his senses and put a stop to things."

"Why would his senses equal him not being with you? If the man has any sense, he'll realize being with you would be the best thing to ever happen to him," he said.

I smiled at the phone. "Orlando, you're sweet. I think I'm afraid he won't be able to let go of our past breakup." I mean, Jordan had compared our breakup to a car crash.

"Soph, it took a literal house fire in the middle of the night to pull him away from you. Even while you were presumably contagious. I don't think you have anything to worry about," he said plainly. "Meanwhile, I'm about to attend church with someone's parents that I've never met, and this girl has yet to agree to accompany me on a date."

"If she has any sense, she'll realize going on a date with you would be the best thing to ever happen to her," I said.

I slid the key into my front door when I heard a familiar truck engine roaring behind me. Jordan's truck pulled up in front of my house.

He cut the engine and kicked open his door while I left the key hanging in mine. I ran from my porch to my gate where he stood.

Eyes worn. Face streaked with charcoal. Clothes smelling of smoke.

"My phone's dead," he said. "I didn't want to wait for it to charge to talk to you."

"How'd it go? It's been hours."

"Took hours to get the fire put out. But it's out. I was out there with Dad, having to answer question after question and deal with stuff." He squeezed the bridge of his nose "It's going to be okay, though. We'll figure it out."

Jordan was always figuring things out. "I'm sorry." I stepped closer to him, my arms crossed. "You should go home and get some sleep. You didn't need—"

"You trying to get rid of me, Rogers?" He raised an eyebrow. The grin tugging at his lips made me feel recklessly hopeful.

I'd made so many choices in my past out of fear, but now, I was ready to make one out of hope.

I grabbed a handful of his sweatshirt in both hands and said, "I love you, Jordan. I've always loved you. I didn't end things with us in the past because of any lack of love. Since I was a girl, I've loved you. I think now as a woman, I love you even more." I'd felt this love for so long it felt like one of my elemental truths. Sophia Rogers was a runner, a teacher, and loved Jordan Silk.

He squeezed my shoulders, his fingertips rough against my skin. "Are you sure you're not just wanting a do-over? Because I'm not interested in the past." He stepped back, still gripping my shoulders and running his eyes down my body. "I want *this* Sophie. The strength, the grace, the confidence... I can't live in this town with you and not call you mine."

"I don't want a do-over." I shook my head. "I don't want to relive our old story, as much as I love it. I want new pages for us."

His forehead pressed against mine.

"Can you forgive me for disappearing on you for years?" I asked because I knew that there was no bridge to the other side of our story if Jordan couldn't trust me.

He pulled his head away from mine and blinked at me, looking at me in disbelief. "*Of course.* I forgave you a long time ago. I knew breaking my heart wasn't your intention. You were a kid trying to survive."

I was standing on the tip of my toes, sliding my arms around his neck. "Well, I'm sorry I ever broke your heart."

He pulled my body tight against his, his big palms warm

against my waist. "I like where we are right now." Then he cleared his throat. "When I drove away last night, I kept asking myself how in the world I was letting anything, at all, tear us apart again. How could I waste any more time not telling you—" His voice broke off.

His pulse throbbed in his neck under my hands.

"Tell me?" I whispered. I'd been desperate to hear what Jordan was thinking.

"Tell you." His voice trembled with emotion. "I've been an idiot since you climbed into the front seat of my truck back in January, thinking I had it in me to be just your friend. Like I had it in me to get over you. 'Cause you asked me if I figured it out, and all I've got, Rogers, is that it's impossible for me to get over you. I never did, and I don't think I ever can."

His lips crashed into mine, dipping me low. I dug my hands into his hair. He dug his hands into my waist.

Every nerve in my body melted under his warmth, as I rasped, "Never get over me then 'cause I'm yours, Jordan."

"All," he kissed me so hard I almost lost my balance, "*mine*."

Chapter 16

DECEMBER 23RD, 2023

I had grown up with a little brother. Someone I could count on to mess up my hair when he walked by, fight me over the last few chips in the bag (or eat the whole bag himself), surprise me with his tenderness right when I needed it most, or make me laugh so hard my abs got sore.

Now, I was about to have sisters. *In a matter of hours.*

I wasn't sure what having sisters looked like. But, for today, it appeared sisters brought champagne and orange juice, fancy curling irons, and makeup to your house. They squeezed into my cramped bathroom with its tiny porcelain sink and lacy curtains to teach me the powers of a good face primer and how to properly curl my hair.

"I grew up in awe of your hair," I said as Jenna twirled a strand of my hair around the curling iron. "Now, I get to see how the magic happens."

"It's taken years to hone my craft." Jenna winked, her own blonde curls bouncy and shiny. "You can always give me a call if you're in a real hair emergency. You know Sarah does."

"I think I relied so long on Jenna's skills that I never developed my own," Sarah said. "I like your fluffy pink bathroom towels." She patted one hanging on the towel rack beside her.

"Thanks," I said, taking in the space. "I can't believe everything is getting packed up."

"We'll be here to help when you get back," Sarah promised, reaching out and giving my arm a squeeze.

"I think we need some music or something. Put on your Christmas playlist, Sarah?" Jenna said.

Sarah opened her phone and after a few clicks, Ella Fitzgerald's "What Are You Doing New Year's Eve" crooned from the speakers. "This is totally your song with Jordan," she said, returning to the outlay of makeup products.

I sipped my mimosa, listening along to the song, so grateful I hadn't given up my one little chance.

Chapter 17

❧

AUTUMN 2023

Summer was sweet as cotton candy and dissolved just as quickly. I had summer break off work, so Jordan and I made up for lost time. It was our own summer bubble, spending lazy warm evenings catching up on the chapters of each other's lives we'd missed.

There were small-town whispers as we met up on Jordan's lunch breaks or walked hand in hand at the Sweet River Summer Festival.

One old high school teacher of ours joked when he got behind us in line at Coffees and Commas, "Have I gone back in time? Am I back in Sweet River High School? It's Sophia and Jordan cuddled up again!"

We didn't care. And mostly, people celebrated.

As we pushed grocery carts through the market or discussed work struggles, it felt good to be doing adulthood arm-in-arm for the first time. It didn't feel like we were picking up from where we left off years ago. It felt like we were growing something new—something made to last. Our years apart made us better partners for each other now, like all along God knew we'd find our way back together and had been preparing us for it.

Months passed of this brand-new bliss until autumn came and our little couple bubble had to burst.

The school year began. Jordan helped me set up my classroom and acquainted himself with my coworkers. We showed up together at football games and potlucks. Our names were a duo in people's mouths again: *Jordan and Sophia.*

Jordan's family had been busy traveling a lot over the summer, so we went from phone calls with his parents here and there to weekly family dinners returning in the fall.

Sitting at their long, walnut family table felt surreal. I was back somewhere so familiar, but it felt so different.

Growing up, the Silk family dinners felt like a cozy, happy place where I got to eat Pat's divine southern cooking, tease Jordan with his siblings, and maybe fall asleep on Jordan's shoulder while we watched a football game in their living room by the fireplace. I always felt like a page in their story, nestled in somewhere I belonged.

Now, I felt anxious.

We started family dinners again in September. During the drive over to the first dinner, I broke out in nervous sweats. I hadn't been to the Silk's house since the funeral, which was such a different situation. This time, I was returning as Jordan's new girl-friend but also his ex-childhood sweetheart.

The air between his sisters and I felt sort of awkward. I wasn't sure.

His parents greeted me with bear hugs. Pat remembered my favorite dip and had set it out as an appetizer.

"Just for you," she said with a wink.

Sarah and Jenna smiled at me when I walked in but kept their distance, barely engaging in conversation. The air was tense.

I knew I could win them over. I was set on winning them over.

But, as fall flew by, and so did family dinners and football games and back-to-school fundraisers with Jordan's nieces and nephews, they kept me at a distance. They were polite, but the warmth from years prior was completely snuffed out. The comfort that was once there was completely gone.

Halloween night, Jordan and I showed up at Jenna's house for trick or treating dressed as a cheeseburger and fries. I skipped up her steps, trying not to bump my red carton into Jordan's big ole bun.

She cocked her head to the side standing in the doorway. Her shiny, blonde hair was tucked behind her ear, as she said, "Oh, I didn't realize Sophie was coming."

"Of course she is." Jordan shrugged. "I've got to spend the holidays with my girl."

Jenna's eyes locked with Sarah's, and even growing up without sisters of my own, I knew the unspoken conversation happening between them.

"I'm sorry. Am I intruding on a family thing?" I offered to try and chip away at whatever ice was between us.

"No, no, it's okay." Sarah brushed the air with her hand as if brushing away my insecurity.

"You're here. You look cute in this little french fry getup." Jenna's smile was devoid of warmth. "Let's get moving," she said to Sarah, and the night went on. The kids tumbled down the front porch steps racing out to trick or treat.

I was sure Jordan had forgotten about that conversation, maybe even Jenna and Sarah had forgotten, but it stayed with me.

One night, Jenna's questioning cocked head returned. In early November, we were at the family dinner table, everyone chattering about Thanksgiving plans, when Pat turned to me. "Well, Sophie, you're coming to the Turkey Trot with us, right?"

The Silks spent every crisp Thanksgiving morning at the Sweet River Turkey Trot. Everyone showing up in Downtown Sweet River bleary-eyed with sneakers on at 8 a.m. on the dot. A man in a giant turkey costume waited to high-five each of us as we crossed the finish line.

I hadn't been in years. Another tradition I was excited to get back.

"Oh, well, yeah!" In my mind, it was a no-brainer. But, after I answered, I felt the awkwardness tighten across the room.

"Definitely." Jordan squeezed my hand.

"You know, I was talking to Jordan the other day about Thanksgiving. Your mom and Orlando are welcome to come with you for dinner." Pat stabbed a bite of broccoli.

"I'll invite Mom and Orlando. I'm not sure if they already have other plans." My eyes shot over to Sarah and Jenna.

They exchanged a loaded glance with each other.

I swallowed air. "Can I bring anything?"

"I usually have the kids bring desserts or sides?" Pat still referred to Jordan and his siblings as "the kids," even though a couple of them had kids now.

"I'll bring an apple pie." My mom had the best recipe.

"A pie sounds perfect," Pat beamed. I wished someone would crack a joke or say they were excited to have me there. Sarah moved food around her plate. The jingle of ice in a glass.

"Never enough pie," Jordan said, stabbing a bite of meatloaf.

"I didn't realize it was already planned that Sophie was coming," Jenna said hesitantly like she wasn't sure she should be saying the words as they left her mouth.

"Of course she is," Jordan said as if the question was laughable. I felt the anxious sweating return, grabbing at my thick sweater.

Pat's brows puckered. "You're surprised?"

"Yeah, it's a *family* thing." Jenna's voice was layered with innuendo.

"Soph is basically family," Westley, Jenna's husband, piped up, waving a fork toward me.

"Are we really doing this?" Cody whispered under his breath.

I stared at my hands in my lap.

"I didn't know new relationships were invited to all the family things now." Sarah crossed her arms and leaned against her chair.

My heart hammered against my chest. I was racking my brain for the exact right thing to say at this moment, but it was agonizingly empty.

"*New relationships?*" Jordan spat out. "Come on."

"Sophie has peed in our pool," Pat said through laughter. "This is the farthest thing from a new relationship."

Sarah sharply inhaled, avoiding my gaze as I glanced across the table.

"I...don't want to intrude?" I said, but I did want to intrude. I chose Jordan and that included his holidays and his family.

"You're not intruding!" Pat leaned in toward the table as she looked at me. "Come and bring your folks."

Why don't you want me there? The question was pounding in my ears. I wanted to ask Sarah and Jenna right then and there. But the conversation steamrolled on, and before I knew it, I was driving back home and dreading Thanksgiving.

My apple pie caught fire. The night before Thanksgiving, after the longest work week ever, my apple pie literally caught on fire.

A couple of days before, I'd been added to the Silk family group chat, and the conversation was dedicated to Thanksgiving meal planning.

PAT

I can make the green bean casserole. I know the right way to do it.

SARAH

you mean you like the way you do it better

JENNA

you mean you like using the canned green
beans

PAT

I don't use canned green beans! But honestly
I don't like to use the ones you use, they're
too crunchy

SARAH

green beans should have crunch

PAT

Not in a casserole, sweetie. It's supposed to
be gooey!

JORDAN

I like it either way, guys

PAT

Then I'll just bring mine then!

JENNA

Okay, okay, I'll bring sweet potatoes.

CODY

ha ha

PAT

What's so funny…You guys don't like my
green bean casserole?

JENNA

That's not it, your way is fine! We just also like
the new way.

PAT

Fine? I've made green bean casserole for
decades.

How are you making the sweet potatoes?

There was no way around except through. I knew I needed to throw my opinions into the group thread if I was going to make any headway. The conversation had moved on to dessert.

JENNA

I can't remember who is bringing what desserts? I'm bringing a pecan pie.

MOM

I'm making my brownies

JENNA

Yesss! YUM!

ME

Hi. I'm bringing an apple pie!

PAT

yes, dear, thank you!

SARAH

I was doing sides and an appetizer. But do we think we need a pumpkin pie? It is Thanksgiving.

JENNA

ooh, yeah, it would be weird without a pumpkin pie.

I am not a baker. But I am a people pleaser.

ME

I can bring both—an apple pie and a pumpkin pie?

PAT

Thanks, you're a doll!

No one else replied.

· · ·

A mere few hours after a Thanksgiving play at school where I had to sweat in a full-body turkey costume, I stood in the kitchen covered in flour, throwing together an apple pie. I was also multitasking researching pumpkin pie recipes on my phone. I barely had time with fall school shenanigans to stop by the market and buy a couple cans of pumpkin puree let alone sit down and find a recipe.

I ran a sweaty, flour-covered hand over my forehead. I regretted agreeing to two pies.

Sliding the apple pie into the oven, I noted it looked a little fuller than usual, but *maybe that meant a thicker, tastier pie.*

As it baked in the oven, I leaned against the kitchen counter scrolling through "easy and quick pumpkin pie recipes" on Google. The keywords were *easy* and *quick*.

I decided on one, perused the pantry, and realized I needed a few extra ingredients, so I shot off a pleading text to Jordan to pick them up on his way over. As I pressed send, I sniffed the smoky air.

I blinked my eyes against my suddenly foggy vision.

A couple of seconds later, it finally clicked, and I dashed toward the oven. It was ablaze inside with fierce oranges and red flames, and in the middle of it all, my apple pie. I screamed and reached for the oven door but then stopped myself. I took a breath, reminding myself, *Do not open the oven door. Do not feed this fire any more oxygen.*

With shaky hands, I turned off the oven and prayed to sweet Baby Jesus to please let the fire burn out quickly. Panicked, I called my mom.

With the phone to my ear, I squinted through the maze of smoke behind the oven door and could see bits of extra filling spilled over the pie dish and into the sides of the oven all ablaze. *It was the extra filling.*

"Mom!" I screamed into the phone. "Mom!"

"Honey?" Mom answered with a tone of surprise.

"My oven is on fire!"

"Honey!" She gasped.

I knelt beside the oven, watching as the fire dimmed, and my pie baked to a blackened crisp. All I could think was, *Now I'd need to ask Jordan for more apples.* I'd promised an apple pie.

"What are you doing? Call 911!"

"It's burning out," I said, staring through the oven door. "I ruined it though." The weight of how much these pies, this Thanksgiving dinner, the Silk family, all meant to me weighed heavy on my chest until I broke under it, crying in a ball on the kitchen floor.

"Sophie. Is it the pies? *What happened?* Do you need me to come over and help you?" Mom said, her voice still high from the panic of hearing her daughter had a small kitchen fire.

I broke into a sob. "I don't have the ingredients for either of my pies. And now I'm making two. Because I just wanted them to like me again."

"Forget about the pies. I'm bringing Nonna's famous tiramisu, so we'll say it's from the both of us." Mom's voice was soft like a hand brushing against a forehead. "And who do you want to like you?"

"All of them. Jordan's family. His sisters can't seem—" I was sniffling into the phone when Jordan walked in through my front door, arms full of grocery bags.

"Rogers, what's going on in here?" His face was a mix of terror and care when he spotted a flour-covered, sobbing me sitting in the midst of a smoke-filled kitchen.

"Mom, I got to go. Jordan's here," I whispered into the phone then ended the call.

Jordan set the bags on the counter. "I take it the apple pie is no more?"

I nodded, swiping at my eyes. "No use crying over spilled apple pie, huh?" I tried to joke. Just Jordan's appearance in my kitchen made things feel a little lighter, a little brighter.

"Two fires in one year—not a good look for us." Jordan

plopped down beside me in the middle of the mess. "What happened here? You look sad. Is it because of the pie?" He peered through the oven door. "Clearly caught fire."

"I am sad, yes. Because I burned the apple pie, and now, I have to remake it. I also have to make the pumpkin pie. I'm also out of apples, and it's getting late. And I was all sweaty in that turkey costume..." I felt a sob try to escape my chest again. "I just want your whole family to..." My voice dropped, barely a whisper as I said, "Love me back."

"You love me. And you love me good. That's all you've gotta do for them to love you." Jordan pulled me close to his side.

"It's not that easy in the world of in-laws," I moaned into his shoulder. He smelled like pine and clean laundry. I burrowed in closer.

"In-laws?" He grinned. "Thinking ahead."

"I know how much your family means to you. So they mean a lot to me." My voice felt small under the weight of my big feelings —my big fears.

"This is about my sisters and their weirdness about your holiday invitations?" Jordan tipped my chin up with his index finger to look into my eyes.

I nodded.

"This is the first holiday in a lifetime of holidays spent together. My sisters will get used to it. Plus, you're easy to love, Rogers. The girls don't stand a chance."

I let out a big breath. Jordan breathed with me.

I grinned at him and swiped a flour-covered finger across his nose. "Are you looking forward to a lifetime of pies on fire and flour everywhere?"

"I'm looking forward to a lifetime of *you*. I want it all. Every version." He pulled me into his lap as he spoke. "Messy flour-covered you. Starting-fires you. Young you. Old you. Crying you. Melting-in-my-arms you. I've loved every version I've known, so keep 'em coming." He ran his fingers through my hair as he pulled my lips against his, kissing me deeply.

My hands left smears of flour across his sweater as we kissed there on the kitchen floor.

He kissed me until I was breathless—until I was giggly and happy. All my stress went up in smoke.

As we stood back up, he said, "Now, put me to work. If you're making pies, then I'm making pies, too."

I winced. "I'm all out of apples. I migh—"

"I got you covered." He reached into one of the paper bags sitting on the counter and pulled out a bag of apples. "I saw these in the baking section and thought, 'Why not have a backup?'"

"You *knew* I would mess up the pie." I gasped.

"No, no." He started to laugh. "But I have seen you in the kitchen, and I know it takes a few—"

I gave him a playful shove. "You had no faith in my pie-making skills."

"You know, I can honestly say, I didn't expect you to catch the pie on fire." He pointed toward the oven and the charred pie inside.

Chapter 18

THANKSGIVING 2023

ORLANDO

happy turkey day, sorry you've fallen in love with a guy in a Turkey Trot family

you got me feeling thankful

that is thankful I'm in bed right now while you're out running a 5k

ME

my greatest wish is you fall in love with someone who wakes you up every morning for a 5k

The air was cold, our breath coming out in misty clouds as Jordan and I jogged up the sidewalks to the Turkey Trot gathering point in Downtown Sweet River. Decorative turkeys and colorful autumn leaves hung from street lamps and shop windows.

"You guys made it!" Pat said as we joined the family's circle. She wrapped an arm around me. Trees with leaves in golds and reds dotted downtown.

"Five minutes to spare!" Carson tapped his watch.

"Ready to build up an appetite?" Cody asked, slapping Jordan on the back in greeting. "Last year, I did it in twenty minutes while Jordan lagged behind at twenty-two minutes. I think this year, the winner should get a whole pie to themselves."

"Well, we were almost down a pie last night!" Jordan let out a low whistle. Everyone's eyes were on us, full of questions.

"How's that?" Pat asked.

"I caught my apple pie on fire last night. I was distracted." I sighed. Looking at Jordan's family, I desperately wanted the walls between us to drop, and I knew, as with any relationship, you had to give what you wanted to receive. So the first step would be to drop my own walls. "Actually, I was overwhelmed. It was a rough work week that had me working late every evening, including yesterday. I was distracted trying to throw the pies together, and I way overfilled my apple pie. So it spilled over while baking...and I had a small oven fire."

Jordan gave me a supportive shoulder squeeze but couldn't hold back his laughter. Cody grimaced. One of Sarah's hands flew over her mouth.

I place my hands over my face. "We were able to clean the oven!" I said muffled through my mittened hands.

"Just took a couple hours." Jordan winced.

"Sophie! You were up last night with *an oven fire*?" Pat's eyes were wide. Fellow Turkey Trotters were swarming around us, ready for the race to begin. Stretching and shouting to other members of their group.

"You know my girl. She cleaned it up and still made two delicious-looking pies last night. And now, she's here today ready to win the race." Jordan was my eternal pep squad of one.

"It was not that smooth." I chuckled. The countdown began from the loudspeakers set up outside of Coffees and Commas.

I glanced up at the stage before noticing Sarah step over to me. "You should've let us know. We could've helped!" she said, touching the back of my arm.

"And after a full day at the school," Pat said, pursing her lower lip. "You could've told us you were too busy to bring any pies. The menu is too stacked as it is."

"I wanted to help," I said. "I really did."

"Did you still make both pies?" Jenna said, eyes downcast. She'd been the one to push for the pumpkin pie. Her husband was running ahead with their little ones in a double stroller they questionably fit in.

I nodded. "After the fire, and the tears, and the cleaning...it was actually kind of fun. Jordan was over to help. It'll be a funny memory now."

A horn bellowed, and the crowd began to move forward, people racing off. I got in position, but Jenna grabbed my hand.

"Wait?" she asked over the noise.

People weaved around us. A few runners shot us frustrated looks. Christmas music was blaring through the speakers downtown.

"You don't need to feel..." Jenna started but stopped. She looked over at Sarah, who was standing beside us. Everyone else had left. "I hate that you spent last night crying and overwhelmed trying to make pies you didn't have time to make because we made you feel..."

The three of us were holding up traffic. "You made me feel like you two really don't want me around," I finished the sentence.

"No, no." Jen shook her head. "We want you around, Sophie."

"It's not a matter of if we like you or not. We were just feeling...hesitant," Sarah said, rubbing her gloved hands together. "I'm so embarrassed we were making you feel bad."

"We were trying to be the flashing yellow light to slow things down, I guess," Jenna said with her shoulders raised apologetically.

"Why?" I said, trying to speak over "Santa Baby" blaring through downtown. My breath was still coming out in foggy bursts. "You don't trust me? Last time, I was eighteen, and I was—"

"It's not that we don't trust you. It's that...you're *Sophia Rogers*. We know firsthand the effect you have on our brother. You've held his heart in the palm of your hands since you were kids. You could crush it." Jenna said.

"You could crush *him*," Sarah said as the song came to an end. Her words were the only thing hanging in the air.

"I won't crush him," I said with my whole chest.

"We know how he feels for you. I mean, come on, we've never seen him more broken than when he thought he lost you." Jen swallowed then added, "And he's never been happier than when you moved back to Sweet River."

"It's because of that, I think we were trying to be cautious. Like we were dealing with dynamite. Mom was almost as ecstatic as Jordan himself, Cody thought it was a given you two would reunite, and there was us. We weren't trying to be rude. Just careful," Jenna said.

"But we were kind of rude," Sarah whispered. "I'm sorry."

"It's not our place to decide if you should be careful or jump in, anyway," Jenna said. "I know that. Maybe it's my mom instinct coming out. I don't know."

"I appreciate it, but trust me, I've given Jordan's heart more thought and consideration than you can imagine. You can breathe easy knowing if I'm showing up to family dinners and Turkey Trots, I'm here to stay," I said.

Both of them nodded, huddling together for warmth.

"We're not pumping the brakes anytime soon. You're just going to have to accept that and *accept me*," I said in the same steady tone I use in the classroom.

"Sophie, you're already accepted!" Sarah exclaimed.

"You're basically family. We'll have your back from now on." Jen leaned her head on my shoulder. "I'm sorry. No more tears over us."

"I'm sorry, too." Sarah leaned her head on my other shoulder.

The Christmas speakers paused, and then, "PLEASE KEEP MOVING IF YOU ARE PARTICIPATING IN THE TROT!" boomed through the speakers. We broke into a giggle and raced off together, running off arm in arm.

Our two families spent Thanksgiving together, sharing food and stories. Mine and Jordan's past, once packed away like an old memory, was now affectionately brought back to life around the Silk's dinner table lined with pumpkins and sunflowers.

My heart felt aglow within my chest as my mom and Pat took turns telling their perspectives of mine and Jordan's first date.

Pat's eyes glistened as she said through laughter, "I heard what sounded like some sports announcer on the TV, but it was coming from the bathroom!" She leaned in closer to the table, enjoying everyone's attention. "I walked back to find Jordan giving himself a pep talk in his bathroom mirror. *'You've known this girl for years, buddy. You know she likes you! You've got this, J Man.'*"

The table howled with laughter, plates of my mom's tiramisu and my unburned pies in front of them.

"J Man?" I said to Jordan, cocking my head to the side.

"Oh, well, I've got one." My mom patted the table. "Remember how they got a flat tire on the way home from prom? I got this late call from them, and I'm rushing to find them, assuming they'll be waiting for me in the car all scared and unsure of what to do. No, not our kids. I drive up the backroad to find the two of them changing the tire *in the mud*—and yes, of course, my daughter with her prom dress hiked up all muddy there on the ground." She shakes her head.

"Prom was over. I could mess up my dress then!" I defended myself.

"Two peas in a pod, these two." My mom's eyes twinkled as she took a sip of her apple cider.

I was thankful for this past outlined in gold, but I was even more thankful for how it led me straight to this future I was stepping into.

Chapter 19

DECEMBER 1ST, 2023

ME

Jordan, send me your Christmas wishlist?

JORDAN

Literally I'm so stupidly happy lately, I can't think of a single thing

just more of what I have now

which means I really just want all the Sophie I can get

ME

that can be arranged

To kick off December, my classroom made gingerbread houses. The kids were giggling and ecstatic which made it seem like a great idea, but they were also messy and hyper, which left me coming back home bone tired. My back was achy. My feet were sore.

The sun set earlier now, so the sky was black outside my window as I watched Jordan's truck roll up outside my house.

"How was gingerbread house day?" Jordan asked as he kissed me hello on the cheek while I checked on my crockpot chili, the spicy tomato scent filling the kitchen.

"Logan said it was the best day ever." I grinned. Logan was quiet and reserved, and it felt good to see him so giddy about something. "So it feels like a success."

Jordan walked over to my dining room table, eyeing the remaining gingerbread kit. "What've we got here?"

"We had one kit left over," I said, placing a wooden spoon on the spoon rest. "Wanna make it?"

Jordan leaned against the oak table, arms crossed over his chest. "Is it flammable?"

"Flammable?" I asked, confused.

Jordan chuckled, and I realized what he was getting at.

"It's not going *in the oven* because the gingerbread is prebaked." I narrowed my eyes. "You don't have to worry about any kitchen fires."

"Hey, hey, you can never be too safe!" Jordan smiled at me, pleased with himself.

"After all the houses I made today, I'm pretty much a pro." I popped my shoulders proudly.

Jordan broke into the cardboard box, pulling out the pieces of gingerbread and bags of gumdrops, candy canes, and frosting, laying them out on the table. I put on a Nat King Cole Christmas album, and the two of us got to work.

"I learned that frosting makes the best glue," I explained as I leaned over the table smearing frosting on the edges of the gingerbread.

Jordan watched me as he kicked back in a dining room chair, a smile tugging at his lips. He tucked a piece of my hair behind my ear.

I stood up and purveyed the walls of the gingerbread house. Jordan was just watching me. Had been the whole time.

"Jordan Silk, you are no help."

"Rogers, I'm building houses all day, looking at walls. When I come home, all I want to look at is you."

"These walls are gingerbread," I said, mindlessly licking frosting off my fingers, his eyes tracking the movement. My heart race quickened.

He placed his hands on either side of my waist. "Gingerbread walls. And a distractingly gorgeous contractor." He tugged me into his lap.

"A handsy assistant," I said.

He weaved his arms around my waist, tucking my back against his chest, his breath against my neck sending goosebumps across my skin.

I attempted to concentrate, placing messy dollops of frosting on the gingerbread roof. I knew I was better than the work I was doing, but Jordan was kissing the back of my neck, leaving a trail of kisses on my shoulder.

"I like the red gumdrops best, you know," he said, his warm breath behind my ear, and I barely understood a word. He reached over and grabbed a red gumdrop I'd stuck to a frosting dollop on the gingerbread door and popped it in his mouth.

My jaw dropped. "Actively working against my efforts now?"

He shrugged sheepishly as he chewed.

I shook my head at him. "I should fire my assistant. He's no help, then eats my doorknob."

"Eh, those doorknobs weren't up to code, anyway," Jordan said, twisting me around in his lap until we were nose to nose. Our breath mingled between us. I pressed into him, his warmth encompassing me. I wanted to live right here, in this spot, forever.

His lips met mine, and it tasted like sugary frosting and felt like home.

DECEMBER 15TH, 2023

"Let's go for a drive," Jordan bypassed a greeting, standing on my front porch. It was a few days into December, and the temperature had plummeted. We were both bundled up in our coats. "I've got a thermos of hot chocolate in the truck."

This man and his thermoses of hot chocolate. I grinned. "You know I can't resist a Christmas lights drive."

We'd gone for our traditional drives with hot cocoa to see the houses strung with Christmas lights since we were sixteen and had finally gotten our driver's licenses, so we had our established Christmas lights routes by now. I was surprised when he turned left from my driveway instead of right.

"Heading to the school?" I asked.

"Heading toward *our house*," he said with a twinkle in his eye that put the decorated houses we passed to shame.

Our house. By that, I knew he meant our mutual dream house. The one we both would park in front of just to think. Or dream.

"As much as we love that place, it is never decorated," I said. No one lived there, so no one ever decorated it.

He turned on the oldies Christmas radio station. "Have Yourself a Merry Little Christmas," pulsed through the speakers.

"Let's drive by anyway. Just to see."

My breath caught in my chest as we pulled up outside the house. It was decorated straight out of a Hallmark Christmas movie—strung with lights, wreaths on the windows and front door, and a pathway of lights lining the sidewalk path to the front porch.

"*Oh.*" My heart sank a little. "Someone bought it."

Mine and Jordan's future didn't need those old dreams to come true. All we needed was each other. Any house would do. I still couldn't help but feel a little ache, knowing someone else would call it theirs now when for so long, we used to joke it was *ours*.

Jordan put his truck in park. "It was about time someone snatched it up."

I grabbed the thermos and took a warm sip. "Let's keep driving. The family inside might feel weirded out with our truck idling out here."

"Let's go say hi and wish them Merry Christmas." Jordan unbuckled his seatbelt.

I scrunched my nose at the idea and shook my head no.

"What? Come on. It's Christmas, Rogers." Jordan tilted his head toward the house.

"Jordan—" I groaned.

"You're basically a neighbor living down the street from them. I think it'd be nice. We can tell them how much this house meant to us." Jordan was so cutely earnest. He somehow convinced me. I hesitantly slid out of the truck into the blustery cool night.

I followed Jordan through the front yard winter wonderland and onto the front porch. Before I could change my mind, Jordan was knocking on the door.

No answer. I tugged on my scarf. Jordan shrugged and said, "Why don't we..." And, to my shock, he pushed the front door open.

"Jordan!" I gasped, looking at him in shock, then turned toward the open door. As my eyes fell toward the entrance, I saw a trail of flickering candles paving a path toward an empty living room.

My eyes were wide and round as I glanced back toward Jordan.

"Follow the candle path," Jordan whispered. "It's for you, Sophie."

As I stepped into the house, I realized the walls were covered like a scrapbook. Pictures from mine and Jordan's childhood growing up together, old notes we'd passed back and forth during classes, medals from runs we'd done together, pictures from proms and formals, from the day he got his first truck, and letters, receipts, and ticket stubs hung on the wall.

There were Christmas lights laced through the memories and a Christmas tree aglow and decorated in the corner of the room.

I walked slowly through the walls of memories around me, my hands grazing the shiny photos or crumbled paper. My mind was spinning. My heart was reeling.

"That," Jordan pointed to an old, yellowing note, "was from before we were together and Andy Dodson was planning to ask you out after school. Do you remember I passed you that note asking you to stay after class and help me with a project? I was terrified of losing you." I remembered that day, his young, nervous energy. "I had good sense even then."

"This is a receipt from one of our Dairy Queen ice cream dates." He started to laugh. "There were piles of ice cream-related receipts."

"We like sweet treats," I said, my voice mystified. Placing my fingers to my lips, I stopped at a photo of young us posing in front of a cabin. "Here we are at summer camp."

Jordan grabbed my hand, pulling me toward the far wall at the back of the room. "This wall here is my favorite."

That wall had photos from this past year—every memory since I'd come back home. He'd printed out some of our early text messages and call logs. The receipt from our accidental Valentine's

Day date. A photo from one of the Saturday morning soccer prac-
tices. Our tickets from the Sweet River Summer Festival.

My hand went straight to my chest, trying to hold myself
together. "Oh, Jordan." I turned to find him on one knee,
kneeling before me lit by candlelight.

"I love our past. What we had. Our foundation," he said,
gesturing toward the walls behind us. "But, Sophie, I'm even
more in love with what we have *right now*. I'm excited about the
two of *us* tomorrow, and the next day, and the day after that. I
want more of this." He pointed to the wall in front of us with the
photos from this year. "*Forever.*"

I collapsed into his arms, kneeling before him, too. "Is this
really happening?" My voice was shaky, my hands were shaky.

He pulled out a little black box and popped it open between
us, inside was a shiny, silver ring. "It's really happening, Rogers. I
talked with the owners of this house, told them our story, and it's
ours if we want it. They like us so much, they even let me cover
this place in Christmas lights and Polaroids."

"It's ours if we want it?" I whispered in a tone of awe. My
heart was about to beat straight out of my chest and into Jordan's
hands.

"Do you want it, Sophie?" He held the ring up higher. "Will
you marry me?"

I nodded, breathless. "Yes," I said, tears falling from my eyes
onto the shiny hardwood floors beneath us. "Yes. I want this
forever, too."

He took my shaking hand and slid the ring on my left finger.
It was sparkly and beautiful, but even more so, it was a tangible
promise, a hopeful sign of what was to come.

"This is a dream," I said, breathless.

"*You're* my dream, Sophie. You always have been. Without
you, none of it matters. It's this," he ran his finger over my
bottom lip, "smile of yours, this heart of yours, the way you keep
me guessin' that makes my everyday life become a dream come
true. I don't want any of it if there's no you."

"Oh, there's a me." I wrapped my arms around his neck, pulling his forehead against mine. The cold air from outside breezed into the room. "You got me *forever* now."

Jordan reached into his back pocket and pulled out mistletoe, twisting it in his fingers before me with a twinkle in his eye. He held it up over the two of us just like he did all those years ago.

I broke into giggles while he pressed his lips against mine— slow and sweet.

"Of course, you had to bring the mistletoe," I said between kisses, grabbing his scarf and pulling him in closer.

He dropped the mistletoe to the ground and slid his hands possessively around my waist, my body flat against his. *Forever* sounded good to me.

Knock, knock. We turned, and there stood his mom and mine in the doorway. I gasped and lifted my left hand to show off my ring. They cheered running toward us, followed behind by the rest of our families. Shoes thudding against what was soon to be our new floors. The faces of those we loved lit by twinkle lights. We talked about getting married in the spring. Maybe April. Maybe May. Ending the night all of us huddled around the front porch.

Past and present mingling together and making something beautiful.

Chapter 21

DECEMBER 16TH, 2023

JORDAN

good morning fiancé

ME

good morning soon-to-be husband

JORDAN

ready to show off that ring at the most happening spot in town??

ME

the Christmas tree lot is the most happening spot in town?

JORDAN

if we're judging by the parking, oh yeah

If you were looking for a fresh, real Christmas tree in Sweet River, the Holly & Ivy Christmas Tree Lot was the place to go. They didn't only sell trees. They had fresh garland and wreaths, a hot chocolate stand, and a Santa with a line of kids weaving down the block. I was looking for a tree, and I'd enlisted *my fiancé* to help me pick and haul it home.

The scent of spruce and fir mingled with cocoa and peppermint hit my senses as we walked onto the lot hand in hand. The ring on my finger sent a little thrill down my spine.

"Okay, we need hot chocolate with marshmallows, stat." I squeezed Jordan's hand.

"Oh, you don't have to tell me. That's exactly where I was headed," Jordan said, his breath coming out in frosty puffs.

We stood in line for the hot cocoa stand, Jordan warming my fingers in both of his hands, when I spotted Emma Brown and Gabriel Hernandez standing amongst the rows of Christmas trees. She had on a floppy Christmas hat over her long blonde hair and was giggling while Gabriel showed her a picture he'd taken on his phone. He had some fancy camera attachment on it.

I turned back to Jordan, who was reading the menu. "Do we need chocolate dip pretzels or roast chestnuts? Or both?"

"Both."

"Hey you two," I heard a familiar voice. Lucy Rhodes, the redheaded kindergarten teacher was in line behind us with her sisters, Gracie and Olivia.

"Hi there," I said. "Looking for a tree?"

"Yeah, Liv and I are roommates, so we're scoping out the perfect tree for our place," Lucy said, nodding her head toward her smaller, freckly older sister.

"All I know is I want it to be poofy, like maybe a spruce or something," Olivia mused, really pondering her tree choices.

"I like 'em tall," I said.

"Obviously." Lucy giggled, eyeing Jordan from her five foot three stature. He had over a foot on her.

I felt my cheeks go pink. "I suppose that's true."

"Can you believe it's been nearly a year since our impromptu group Valentine's dinner?" Lucy asked as we stepped forward in line. "And look where you are now."

I lifted my left hand and wiggled my ring finger. Lucy's jaw dropped. We both started to squeal. "He asked last night!"

Suddenly, Jordan and I were wrapped up in the arms of all three Rhodes sisters.

"A happy couple looking for a Christmas tree!" A cheerful man with a long silvery beard found us amongst the rows of fir trees later. "My name's Richard and I'm happy to assist you. What size are you thinking?"

"The tree is for Sophie here. All she's given me is she wants it tall, green, and smelling like Christmas." Jordan shook the guy's hand.

"The smelling like Christmas is the real non-negotiable," I explained.

Richard nodded seriously. "Let's talk the dimensions of your living room," Richard said, eyeing the trees around us. "You might like a tall tree, but what's your ceiling height?"

Jordan started answering with information about the living room in my rental... but all I could imagine was our new home. The one we were going to fix up together. The one we'd always dreamed about.

I imagined the two of us wrapping a tree in golden lights in the living room where he proposed.

But I didn't want it to live only in my imagination.

"I've got a popular one this way." We followed Richard down a grassy path. Jordan excitedly grabbed my hand.

I was so much more than ready for our future together. I wanted it to start *right now*.

I didn't want to spend the holidays as anything but his wife. I was ready for Christmas mornings in our dream home and Valentine's Day mornings whispering *husband* in his ear.

We'd waited long enough to find our way back to each other. Why spend any more of our time together waiting?

I was having this epiphany as Richard chatted tree dimensions with Jordan. I swallowed.

"Actually, could we have a few minutes to talk it over?" I interrupted the two of them.

"Sure, sure. Come find me when you're ready," Richard said before walking off in the shadow of plush pines.

I turned to Jordan, fixing my eyes on his and hoping he was feeling what I was feeling. "I was just thinking...doesn't it feel silly to buy a Christmas tree for anywhere other than our dream home?"

He jutted out his chin in consideration. "I'm listening."

"I know the place is a fixer-upper, but it's definitely livable." I put my hands in my coat pockets.

"You want to move into the new house before Christmas?"

"It's more than that, honestly. I want to wake up Christmas morning with my husband."

Jordan's brows shot up. "Rogers, I'm your husband whenever you want me to be your husband."

"Should we call over Richard? See if he's ordained?" I stood on my tiptoes, pretending to look around for him.

"So you're saying you don't want to wait until spring?"

"I'm saying I don't want to wait until the New Year." I felt excitement bubbling up from my toes to my ears.

Sweet River was having its grand Christmas tree lighting downtown in front of city hall. Coffees and Commas was open late for the occasion so people could have warm cinnamon scones and gingerbread hot chocolate as they waited for the ceremony. Sweet River Orchestra was playing Christmas music on the city hall lawn under a sky of winter stars.

Like two giddy kids in love, Jordan and I raced down the sidewalks, trying to find our families. City Hall had thick garland sloped across the front windows.

Everyone had arrived earlier than us. We'd gotten distracted gleefully planning our wedding. We'd agreed on the location in seconds, so I'd made a few calls to secure it while Jordan and Richard strapped the tree to the top of our truck. Then when we went to drop off the tree at our new house, we got caught up in figuring out all the details.

Jordan spun me around in the living room of *our* house, his big hands under my fluffy coat. "We're really doing this."

My mom spotted me in the bustling downtown crowd waving her hand in the air. "Sophie!" she called out.

The rest of the crew turned to see us.

"Next week? Is this really happening?" Pat nearly shouted as Jordan and I walked up.

Sarah's eyes were wide. "I thought your text message was a joke at first!" She bit her lip. "But then when I thought about it, it actually makes perfect sense."

"You said in your message you guys already got the location?" Jenna asked, holding a plastic cup to her mouth.

I nodded excitedly.

Orlando hung an arm around my shoulder. "I'm Brother of Honor, right?"

"We decided on that when we were kids," I said into his shoulder. We pulled apart, misty-eyed. "I have to have you there beside me."

"So this is happening," my mom said, as the music came to a stop. "You're getting married *in a week*."

"This is happening," I whispered. The Christmas music faded away, and the countdown began. Our Sweet River mayor held a red button in his hand.

"We have a week to plan a wedding." She covered her face with her hands.

"A Christmas wedding," Sarah added. "I love it." She sighed wistfully.

"Three, two," people shouted while Jordan slipped his arms around my waist from behind, tugging me against the warmth of his chest on this cold night.

The crowd cheered, "One!" and just like that, the twelve-foot tree was lit with glowing, multicolored lights in the center of downtown. The orchestra began to play "O Christmas Tree," as everyone clapped and cheered.

I hadn't felt so sure in a long time that I was exactly where I wanted to be.

Chapter 22

DECEMBER 19TH, 2023

I took Jenna, Sarah, Pat, my mom, and of course, my man of honor, with me to try on wedding dresses.

"I've heard the best things about this place. I even follow them online," Sarah said as we pushed open the glass door to the shop. She'd been the one to send me the name of this shop, the Blushing Bride, and told me she'd made an appointment.

When deciding to plan my wedding in a week, I'd forgotten about the tiny detail of finding a wedding dress in a week. My wedding crew consisted of our family members: Pat and Mom were on the guest list, Orlando was our DJ and food guy, Sarah and Jenna were handling flowers and décor, and everyone filled in any other need that arose.

One of the last needs: the dress. I felt thankful for Sarah refusing to let me let it fall between the cracks—shaking her head vehemently *no* when I joked that I could always just wear a big white fluffy coat and earmuffs.

"I'm thinking I want something that leans into the wintry, Christmas feeling of December," I explained to the stylist.

"Oh, and you said you wanted beaded detailing," Jenna added, reaching her hand to mine and giving it an encouraging squeeze.

I nodded.

The stylist, Cleo, a younger woman with big brown eyes, pursed her lips and said, "I have a couple of dresses that I think might be perfect."

She walked away, and I looked to everyone finding their seats around the trio of mirrors. Mom was already tearing up as she had been for the past few days, and I hadn't even tried on a single dress yet.

"Mom!"

"I'm okay. I'm okay," she sniffled. "I just still think of you in your dress-up tutus and messy ponytails, and now here we are... buying a wedding dress."

Now nearly everyone was sniffling.

Only Orlando, who was sipping one of the free flutes of champagne, had dry eyes.

"Do you guys like the flower dress we picked?" I asked Jenna since her daughter was our flower girl. We'd tried on the dress last night, but I wanted to double check she liked it.

"Are you kidding? I had to negotiate with her to not have her wear it today. She adores it. I love the snowflake-like lace on the front and the red bow on the back," Jenna said, then held out her phone to me. "Look at this picture of her in the dress and your little ring bearer trying on his tiny tux."

Cleo walked in with a rack of dresses, but it was the one hanging in the front with the sheer, beaded sleeves and neck with snowflake-like beading on the skirt that caught my breath.

I had to try it on right away.

And like with my engagement—I knew instantly and didn't need much time to decide. I twirled in the dress, turning to everyone. "This is the one."

"Sophie." Jenna clutched her chest.

Sarah's jaw was hanging open.

Mom was in tears, while Pat said, "Oh, Sophie."

My eyes landed on Orlando. His eyes were soft on me. He blinked a couple of tears away and said, "This *is* the one."

. . .

As we drove back home to Sweet River, going over our wedding to-do list with Jordan on speakerphone, he asked, "Is there anything else my bride wants?"

Sarah giggled, and Orlando rolled his eyes next to me in the backseat. "Everything has come together better than I'd hoped." Then, without even realizing I felt this way I added, "The only thing that would make it any more perfect would be if it snows."

"I'll add it to the list." Jordan's voice boomed through the speakers.

I wrapped my hands up in my buttery scarf.

"That'd be beautiful, Sophie," Jenna said dreamily.

"But you know fickle Texas. It hasn't snowed in December since—" Mom started.

"Since I was fifteen," I said, watching houses twinkling with Christmas lights zip by the car window.

Jordan and I walked home from school on a cold, windy December day. I was wrapped up in a heavy coat with my nose going numb. It was late afternoon. The light was growing dim under gray skies as we trailed through our neighborhood streets.

I'd been telling Jordan how my family had been so busy lately. We hadn't even decorated for Christmas yet, and I was wishing for it to feel like Christmas.

"Let's get into your garage and grab some of the decoration boxes. I'm sure your mom won't mind. She might even be glad to have the help."

"You're probably right," I said when something cold and wet plopped on my cheek. We both stopped in our tracks and glanced up to see millions of tiny flurries falling from the sky.

"Snow?" I gasped.

"Snow." Jordan nodded, his hazel eyes bright. We held out our hands and let the snowflakes land on our mittens.

It was quiet in the neighborhood. No one was outside, except the two of us, Jordan and me, the only ones witnessing this snowfall. Like we were the only ones let in on the surprise.

Flurries started falling harder, and I squinted up to the sky as they landed across my face, cold and light. I giggled, opening my eyes to Jordan. His nose was pink. He grabbed my hand and pulled me a couple of steps closer.

"It's like we're in a snow globe."

"I wouldn't mind getting trapped in a snow globe with you." I grinned up at him. He brushed his rough fingertips across my lashes, my cheeks, my lips, everywhere the snow landed. My body flooded with warmth on this frigid afternoon.

I snuck my hands under his old coat worn by his dad, now him, and sometimes, me. It was heavy and warm over me as I nestled my cheek against his solid chest. His heartbeat was against my ear. He wrapped that coat around my shoulders like a blanket. We stood like that for a while. I lost track of time.

Snow fell around us quietly like a winter whisper, as Jordan said, "I love you, Sophie. I think I always have."

I rested my chin on his chest, looking up at him. "I love you too." I felt that love so deeply I'd bit back saying it for months now, waiting for the right moment. I knew we were just teenagers, but I also knew what we had was rare and magic like a surprise snowfall on a December day in Texas.

He kissed my forehead before I buried my face in his chest again with a contented sigh, thinking if I could relive a moment over and over, this would be the one.

Chapter 23

DECEMBER 21ST, 2023

I'd attended a few of the Silks' Annual Christmas parties back when we were dating. It was a big deal that I got invited back then since it was a big tradition for Jordan's cousins and aunts and uncles, and his dad's cousins and aunts and uncles, and some of *their* cousins and aunts and uncles. Honestly, for most of the parties, I was just trying to remember people's names and how they were related to Jordan.

Every December 21, all the extended relatives come to a big Christmas reunion party. It was a big deal if someone brought a date. It was an even bigger deal to attend the day before our wedding. Especially our last-minute wedding that we'd invited people to only six days ago.

This big party always took place at Uncle Andy's house. He was a cotton farmer with a big farmhouse with more than enough room to fit everyone. He had a patio perfectly styled for entertaining, a tennis court that people danced on and where kids played Red Rover, and a pool that the teenagers were always daring each other to dive into. Jordan dove in once when he was twelve and wound up with a cold that Christmas.

We walked inside, and before we'd taken two steps into the

entryway, his Aunt Belinda squealed, "There's the bride-to-be!" immediately scooping me into a hug.

"White Christmas" crooned through the speaker system, there were ten-foot trees plopped around the house with shiny red and green bulbs, garland looped over the windows, and people were lined up at tables full of potluck dishes. Kids raced around underfoot.

"You hungry, Rogers?" Jordan asked over the hum of Christmas music and chatter.

"Always." I pointed toward the line for food.

In line, we were asked about the wedding. Then over heaping plates of brisket and baked mac and cheese, we retold the story of how we got back together a few times to a few different people. We were really perfecting how to tell it, and throughout the day, people who couldn't make the wedding were slipping us congratulatory cards.

Near the end of the party, everyone congregated around the shiny black piano in the family room with tall windows and even taller ceilings, to sing Christmas carols. My back was against Jordan's torso with his arms crossed over my chest. We were belting out "The First Noel," and I had to repress a chuckle because this was like something out of a Christmas movie, this tradition of theirs.

But then, I realized it was *my* tradition now, too. This was *my* Christmas party now. I'd be invited every year. Today, I was getting a glimpse into the loud, delicious, slightly rambunctious, cheesy future. My kids—our kids—would one day spill hot chocolate on Uncle Andy's couch and wrap Aunt Melinda up in a big hug as she breathed in their sweet toddler smell and help me carry in trays of Christmas cookies I'd made for the potluck.

I nestled in deeper against him, and he let out a grumbly hum I could feel through his chest.

"You ready to go?" he whispered.

"Let's stay for one more song."

Chapter 24

DECEMBER 23RD, 2023

AUNT SUE

Snow??

AUNT FRANCES

Is this weather okay with your outdoor
wedding???

ME

It's more than okay!

Better than if I planned it myself.

I woke up the morning of my wedding to a rare December snowfall in Sweet River, Texas. The grass and trees outside were blanketed in fresh, glistening snow. Like a wedding gift from God himself.

Our impromptu wedding was supposed to be small and intimate, but we both kept inviting people we ran into throughout the week, especially during the Silk Christmas party. I peeked out my mini blinds into the snow-laden park across the street. It was bursting with over half of Sweet River.

The park where last spring Coach Jordan asked Miss Sophia to have coffee with him was now filling with our friends and family to watch us say *I do* as the sun set low in the sky.

Chairs were looped with twinkle lights. The aisle was lined with flickering lanterns and a trail of white rose petals that led to Jordan. Our childhood pastor stood at the end of the aisle. Half of his laugh lines were caused by our childhood antics. An old friend strummed a guitar as people took their seats, and the first of the wedding party gathered at the end of the aisle.

As I looked out at the wedding waiting across the street, my breath hitched in my throat. In minutes, I'd be walking across those petals to Jordan. I let the blinds snap closed, placing my hand against my heart to steady myself.

"Sophie girl, are you ready?" my dad asked, appearing in the doorway to my bedroom. "We're almost up."

Tears brimmed in my eyes as I said, "I'm *so* ready." I could run down that aisle.

I clutched a bouquet of red and white roses to my chest as my dad walked beside me, Jordan's eyes latched on mine the entire time. The two of us wavered between crying and laughing as I made my way down the petal-laden path.

"What Are You Doing New Year's Eve?" strummed softly in the background.

My mom beamed on the front row, catching my eye and mouthing, *I love you.* I watched Jordan and his mom exchange a smile. His sisters stood beside me in red silk dresses and soft white coats.

As I took my spot across from Jordan, Orlando placed a hand on my shoulder from behind me and gave it a reassuring squeeze.

The sun was setting, putting a chill in the air, as Jordan and I promised every Christmas, every New Year, every season, every up and down, every single kiss, every loss, every victory, every moment that we could, to each other.

When our pastor said, "Now you may kiss the bride," Jordan slid his arms around my waist and dipped me. The crowd applauded, and the music started back up. I could feel his smile against my lips as we kissed. That smile was mine forever.

Epilogue

CHRISTMAS MORNING, EIGHT YEARS (AND THREE KIDS AND TWO DOGS) LATER

"MOM! DAD! SANTA LEFT ME A BIKE!" A little six-year-old voice shouted from downstairs.

I yawned sleepily and turned into Jordan's chest.

"It's still dark out," Jordan mumbled. "How can he already be awake, at," he shot a glance at the clock on our nightstand, "five-thirty a.m."

"That's even after we caught him sneaking downstairs to try and catch Santa at eleven." I giggled into his chest. "Hopefully, Mikey doesn't wake up Hannah."

"Mommy?" Our four-year-old girl stood in our doorway. "Is it Christmas yet?"

"Yeah, baby girl, it's Christmas morning!" Jordan said, opening his arms up to Hannah as she ran and jumped into his arms. She snuggled into his chest.

We heard the thud of Mikey's feet running up the stairs. "Be careful, Mikey," I called out.

Mikey ran into our bedroom with a stocking in his hands. "Guys, come on, you've got to see what Santa left—and he ate all the cookies. Every one of 'em!"

I pulled myself up onto my elbows. "I bet he worked up an appetite carrying around your big boy bike."

Mikey sighed happily. "It is big."

"We've got to get out on it today, huh?" Jordan said after giving Hannah a kiss on her curly head.

Hannah crawled across the bed toward me. "Does Baby Brother know it's Christmas, Mommy?"

"I don't know." I looked down at my big pregnant belly poking out over the ivory duvet. "Should we tell him?"

Hannah placed a hand on either side of my belly. Her messy chestnut curls fell over her face. "Merry Christmas, Baby Brother! Hope you get to be here soon. You'll *love* Christmas!"

I swept Hannah up into my arms, wrapping her little body over my stomach and giving her a kiss. "He can't wait to meet his big sister."

"And brother!" Mikey added from his spot by the foot of the bed.

Jordan caught my eye, sneaking his hand over to mine and giving it a squeeze.

The four—and a half—of us scrambled down the stairs. The kids poured out their stockings while Jordan poured us mugs of coffee. I nestled into the couch by the twinkling Christmas tree, remembering standing in this very living room when it was empty of everything except memories taped onto the walls and Jordan down on one knee.

Over the years, these walls have seen it all.

How Jordan carried me into the living room in my wedding dress and kissed me breathless on the floor. How we painted each room and refinished the floors that spring.

Or the hours I labored with Hannah, pacing the living room floors in circles.

Mikey took his first steps on these floors.

Our first family photos were framed and hanging on the walls in the spot where Jordan had hung up our camp photos the night he proposed to me.

I'd known eight years ago that I couldn't wait to start this life with Jordan, not even a few months. I wanted it all with him and as soon as possible. I watched my kids playing with their Christmas gifts in front of the tree, and Jordan carrying the coffee over to me and thought, *This was what I couldn't wait to begin. I'd take as much of this life with this man as I could get.*

Jordan handed me the steaming mug, and said "Merry Christmas, Rogers," planting a kiss on my forehead.

Our baby boy gave a swift kick, and I quickly placed a hand on my stomach. "Guys, he's kicking! I think he wants to say Merry Christmas!"

Coming Soon

Olivia and Victor's story coming in 2025
(if you don't know who that is, go read *Lucy Loves Him Not* right
now!)

Acknowledgments

I'm going to try and keep this short and sweet like this novella. But, there are a few people I have to mention!

Thanks to God who is all about hope, healing and love that understands and persists... like the love found in this story.

Joseph, my husband, I couldn't write a word without you. And just like Sophie, I couldn't wait to start this life with you.

Ivy (who is starting to read, so I know you'll see your name and squeal!) and Sutton, thank you for being my biggest cheerleaders.

A special thank you to those who read *One Little Chance's* pages at their earliest and helped me make this story what it is now. Mom (so thankful I was born to a bookworm), Jenna, Hannah Marie, Ashley, and Erin. I also have to thank my mother in law for reading it early (even though it made her cry on a plane). And Abby and Rachael for talking with me about Sophie and Jordan all the time and brainstorming just the right nickname — "Rogers."

HUGE appreciation to the "team" behind this book: Crystal Nielsen you are a real blessing in my life, Jen Boles your editing is part of what makes Sweet River so sweet, and Melodie Jeffries your skill and creativity brought the Christmas magic.

A special and heartfelt thank you to my readers — and my "core" team— sharing my stories with *you* (especially a cozy little Christmas story) is a gift. I'm so happy my stories found their way into your hands.

www.ingramcontent.com/pod-product-compliance
Lightning Source LLC
Chambersburg PA
CBHW031517010826
48973CB00013B/2639